"Gonçalo M. Tavares burst onto the Portuguese literary scene armed with an utterly original imagination that broke through all the traditional imaginative boundaries. This, combined with a language entirely his own, mingling bold invention and a mastery of the colloquial, means that it would be no exaggeration to say—with no disrespect to the young Portuguese novelists writing today—that there is very much a before Gonçalo M. Tavares and an after . . . I've predicted that in thirty years' time, if not before, he will win the Nobel Prize, and I'm sure my prediction will come true. My only regret is that I won't be there to give him a congratulatory hug."

—Nobel Prize-winning author José Saramago

"It is around the absence of happiness, in the void filled so treacherously with the stagnation brought on by wealth or madness, that Gonçalo M. Tavares constructs his fabulous *Jerusalem*, a book at once evocative of the ghost of Kafka, German expressionist cinema, and the canvases of Anselm Kiefer . . ."

—Helena Vasconcelos

Jerusalem

Originally published in Portuguese as *Jerusalém* by Editorial Caminho, SA, 2005
Copyright © Gonçalo M. Tavares, 2005 by arrangement with Literarische Agentur Dr.
Ray-Güde Mertin Inh. Nicole Witt e. K., Frankfurt am Main, Germany
Translation copyright © Anna Kushner, 2009
First English translation

Library of Congress Cataloging-in-Publication Data

Tavares, Gonçalo M., 1970-
[Jerusalém. English]
Jerusalem / Gonçalo M. Tavares ; translated [from the Portuguese] by Anna Kushner.
-- 1st English translation.
p. cm.
ISBN 978-1-56478-555-8 (pbk. : alk. paper)
I. Kushner, Anna. II. Title.
PQ9282.A89J4713 2009
869.3'5--dc22
2009021380

Partially funded by a grant from the Illinois Arts Council, a state agency,
and by the University of Illinois at Urbana-Champaign

The publication of this book was partly supported by the
DGLB—Direcção-Geral do Livro e das Bibliotecas / Portugal

www.dalkeyarchive.com

Cover: design and composition by Danielle Dutton, illustration by Nicholas Motte
Printed on permanent/durable acid-free paper and bound in the United States of America

Jerusalem

by Gonçalo M. Tavares
translated by Anna Kushner

Dalkey Archive Press
Champaign & London

1

Ernst Spengler was alone in his attic apartment, getting ready to throw himself out the already-open window, when the telephone rang. Once, twice, three times, four, five, six, seven, eight, nine, ten, eleven, twelve, thirteen, fourteen. Ernst answered.

Mylia lived on the first floor at 77 Moltke Street. Sitting in an uncomfortable chair, she was thinking about the essential words in her life. *Pain*, she thought, *pain* is an essential word.

She'd already had one operation, then another, four operations in all. And now this—this echo deep in the center of her body. Being sick, she told herself, is a test, a way to teach yourself how to endure pain. Or else: it's a manifestation of your desire to get closer to Almighty God. And churches are closed at night.

Four in the morning on May 29th. Mylia couldn't sleep. The pain was constant, coming from her stomach—or maybe lower. Where exactly was it coming from? Maybe from her womb. The only thing she knew for sure was that it was four in the morning and she hadn't slept a bit. She couldn't close her eyes because she was afraid of dying.

She got up. Mylia was thin but strong. She didn't waste time on trivialities. (She was always telling herself: don't waste time on trivialities.) She paid attention to things. She knew she had only a few years left to live. The disease had already begun its work: we'll be together for a few years, then the disease will stay and I'll go. She focused her energy on whatever time she had left in her body, and directed it—her energy—like a rolling pin. Poised to roll. *No more trivialities.* Only spend your time on necessities—ignore the insubstantial; the only things that matter are the essentials, the things that really change you, that make everything different, the things that strike you down. Everything should be that way—every single thing you do each day should feel powerful, significant. Mylia looked at herself in the mirror. I'm alive and I've made a mistake. To be sick is to have made a mistake. Maybe even a diabolical mistake. But: sickness does change you. Sickness makes everything different.

So, that day, at four in the morning, Mylia decided to leave her house. The pain hit her differently at night—it was more of a gradual sensation, like watching some kind of chemical goo creeping down a slight incline, its progress barely perceptible to the eye. Day and night aren't on a level playing field. There's a bit of a slant.

Focusing on her pain, in that nonspecific place—somewhere between her stomach and her womb—Mylia went outside, looking for a church.

There's a bum, and he's a little startled. He says he doesn't know. A church? Don't you know what time is it? he asks. You're going to get yourself mugged. You shouldn't be out looking for a church, you should be looking for a cop to walk you home. Why are you even out at this time of night? I could mug you myself!

Mylia smiled and walked on. Her pain was more urgent than their conversation.

I don't want the police, I want a church. Are they really all closed at this hour?

Her feet felt like they weren't part of her. It was clear, though, that her shoes—flat shoes, men's shoes—still went wherever her feet wanted them to. Bones and muscles have a will of their own. Not shoe leather. Shoes must obey, without question. Yes—shoes, obey, Mylia muttered. All matter can be divided into two basic categories: things that move according to their own will, and those that must obey without question (you could say much the same thing about people). Shoes were an example of pure obedience, and as such, they disgusted her. Revolting: the subservience of the material world in relation to man. Not even a dog was as submissive as a shoe.

And yet, there was no possibility of dialogue between the two camps . . . not "enemy camps," really, since this would suggest that there might be some likelihood of their going to war, meeting on the field of battle, marshaling their various forces . . . no, these weren't two predators pecking at each other in order to secure some choice piece of territory, but absolute passivity on one side confronted by pure energy on the other . . . an energy that's just as likely to be destructive as creative, but which, in any case, never stops evolving. No, we aren't the sort of stuff that just sits around and waits, Mylia told herself, walking with determination toward a church.

"The church is closed. Do you have any idea what time it is? It's almost five in the morning. You shouldn't be out here anyway. This is a bad neighborhood at night. It's dangerous."

Mylia felt like laughing in the man's face, good intentions and all. Dangerous! Dangerous for someone as sick as her? Dying from a disease down deep inside her, with only a year or two left? Death was already closing in on her—now she *wanted* danger, something to excite her, wanted to feel something new. She wanted to tell him, this man, he seemed to be a caretaker or something, yes, she was tempted to say, Look, if it's dangerous, then it's not a bad neighborhood at all! At least things can actually *happen* here!

Danger raises questions, calls for immediate answers. What I need is a good question, Mylia thought. A specific question, a question that'll force me to come up with a meaningful response. My sickness isn't an old wolf—it won't run away at the first sign of trouble. No, it's not a frightened wolf prowling around me. It can't just be chased away.

"I don't care about danger," is what she actually says. "I just wanted to visit the church."

"It's five in the morning. Everyone's sleeping. This neighborhood is dangerous. You should go home. Look, come back in the morning. We'll all be rested, and then you'll find whatever it is you're looking for. Please, listen to me. We're all tired."

Mylia was quiet for a while, and then she doubled over thanks to the strange new pain shooting out laterally from the other, familiar, constant pain from near her stomach. Then, yet another new pain announced itself—higher up.

"Excuse me," she said. "I'm in pain."

"You should go home. It's very late."

Mylia composed herself. She asked, "Do you know if there are any churches still open?"

2

The man said goodnight. Mylia walked away. Everything was locked-up tight. Even the little side door. Might as well be a prison. Mylia started walking around and around it.

They were doing some kind of construction on top of the church—during the day men would climb around to work on it. Tiptoeing with bricks, thought Mylia. She'd made herself smile. What kind of job is that, anyway? Climbing all the way up there just to push a brick a few inches higher.

And there was something else making Mylia smile. And blush. She had to pee. But it was after five in the morning. All the doors were closed. That nice man (or maybe he wasn't so nice? . . . maybe all he cared about was making sure nothing untoward happened to his church?) had told her so. That insignificant man had apologized for the church being closed. Mylia understood how the world worked: a man whose job is to apologize to strangers at five in the morning is almost as low as you can get. They must have him cleaning the church toilets, she thought—and then was sorry she'd called that image to mind.

But none of this was what had made her blush, exactly. What had made her blush was the realization that her bladder was full, and that there was no one nearby to see her. She thought: if I were a proud man, a man who didn't care what the world thought of him, I would just lean toward the wall, take my penis out, and do my business right here. What had made her blush was the realization that she wanted to urinate on the church wall.

It wasn't because she wanted to mark her territory, like a dog, outside this place she'd been forbidden to enter. It wasn't because of spite, either—it wouldn't be an act of defiance, a way of protesting the church's hours, which, sadly, hadn't suited her needs that night. No, it was nothing like that. Mylia was about to turn forty; she didn't do things just to be provocative. And she was sick, too; she had to conserve her energy; any action Mylia took would be for Mylia and Mylia alone. I act for myself, she said. I act as though alone in front of a mirror. In the end, everything is about myself. About controlling my impulses.

To be clear: her desire to urinate on the church wall wasn't exhibitionism. It was the image itself that seduced her: the image of homo erectus, human in its most biological sense—a man standing straight with his penis in his hand, pissing against the church wall—this image pursued Mylia and, in a way, made her jealous. She'd never once regretted being a woman, never once tried to do anything "masculine," but at that moment—in a strange, unnecessary, irrational way—she was angry that she couldn't be the man in her image. She felt like a failure.

Of course she knew peeing against the church wall in the middle of the night would be ridiculous. How would she even position herself? Facing the wall or turning her back to it, leaning her ass against the wall, bending over? Any of the available options would force her to bow slightly forward, and it was this "slight" bow that bothered her most. A person should either bend over completely—even throwing herself on the ground, if necessary: there's no shame in cowardice—or else stand up straight, unwavering. Here she couldn't do either: she'd piss on her socks if she tried. Yet her other option, to slink away and leave the wall dry, felt humiliating—like admitting she wasn't up to her image.

And then another image popped into her head. If someone saw her peeing on the church wall, he would think: this person is out of her mind . . .

Mylia had her share of minor anxieties. For example: she was frightened—like so many people she knew—by mice. Completely overwhelmed by an inexplicable hysteria every single time one of these little gray monsters crossed her path. But her true fear, her greatest fear, was of confrontation. She'd kept away from it all her life. If there was even a hint of conflict in the air, she'd tell herself: "They"—whoever *they* were—"could tear me apart . . ." and then she'd run away. She would only go up to people when she was sure she was safe. Escorted by a friendly hand. She could never understand the men and women who actually preferred open aggression, even physical violence, over other forms of conflict.

So it was important to Mylia that she not seem crazy. Of course, after their initial error (look at that lunatic!), any chance witnesses to her wall-peeing would presumably come to their senses and realize that Mylia wasn't crazy after all; that, really, what she was doing was perfectly normal. But the possibility that someone might think, even for a moment, that she wasn't in her right mind—it was too much for her. She thought: I won't let anyone call me crazy ever again.

3

Mylia retreated. She wasn't about to put herself in that position, wasn't about to let anyone think she wasn't in control. Certainly not for the relatively minor prize of peeing against the church wall. She stepped back about ten meters towards a small garden. Leaning back against a tree, she let go.

There was no one around. The pain was still there by her stomach. She bent over, grabbed some grass, wiped, pulled up her underwear, and collected herself.

The church, silent, faced her as before. The sun would rise in less than three hours, and its brightness would be intimidating, a material threat. The church was closed because it was still nighttime, but Mylia wouldn't make the mistake of being seen there in the morning, still wandering around hopelessly. Her moment of weakness with the man who'd opened the church door had been humiliation enough; now Mylia was starting to recover her animal instinct—she would only let herself be seen in a position of strength. She knew this instinct well . . . you could even say she knew it too well, since her sickness as much as her anxiety had always forced her to avoid people when she felt most helpless: when the pain was at its worst, she preferred to be alone. To be seen as weak, she knew, was tantamount to giving up one's membership in the species. Even knowing that she'd probably be dead in a few months—a year would be too much to hope for, she decided—she refused to give up being human. Pride, she often told herself—never lose your pride.

In the meantime, she'd started feeling something new in her stomach. The sensation confused her: it wasn't her pain, it was something else, equally sharp, perhaps even sharper . . .

How ridiculous. I'm hungry, she thought. I haven't eaten for hours. She even considered laughing. I thought I was alone here at night, but my stomach came along . . . it's keeping me company.

This additional pain was cause for reflection, even a certain inexplicable fear. The new pain in her stomach, brought on by hunger, that pain was actually stronger now than the other pain, the constant pain of her sickness, the pain that was at the root of all her fears, big and small. How is it possible, Mylia asked herself, that this pain brought on by needing to eat can hurt me even more than my usual pain? But I already know I'm going to die from the smaller pain . . . the doctors guaranteed it.

She understood then that there, right there, next to the church, her two pains were trying to outdo each other: the pain that would kill her, the bad pain, as she called it, the sickness pain, and, on the other hand, the good pain, the hunger pain, the pain of wanting to eat, a pain that signified life, the pain of existence, as she would say; as though her stomach, even in the dead of night, was the one obvious sign of her humanity . . . and likewise of her rather ambiguous relationship with the things in the world she still couldn't understand. Yes, she was alive, and this proof of being alive hurt even more, at this moment, in an objective and physical way, than the pain she knew was going to kill her. As if, tonight, it was more important to have a bite of bread than live forever.

Mylia looked around: where can I get something to eat at this time of night? Not a single light. No one to be seen.

4

She circled the church again. Still no lights on anywhere. Proof that the world was either dead or still waiting to be born.

Her empty bladder was an unexpected comfort. At least one pain had been dealt with, she told herself, as though this night was a kind of game, a contest she'd been entered into without having realized it, a competition that kept setting little problems in her path—or, rather, in her body—not puzzles but pains, material problems, concrete riddles inside her own body. She had already solved one: she had emptied her bladder next to the tree. One less pain. Her urine had spilled out. The less urine, the less pain in her body.

But that still left all the other pains, and she knew that one of them at least couldn't be solved at all. It came down to one all-important word; the doctors had used it in front of her: there's nothing to be done for this, they said, we have to hope for a *miracle* . . .

It had been a shock. She'd presented her problem to her doctors—a pain, she was ill; it was exactly their kind of problem, an organic complication—and the doctors had responded by shrugging their shoulders sadly (it was a more or less professional sadness) but taking no action, suggesting no therapy: there's no cure for this. Your illness can't be treated. She'd brought her problem to a bunch of doctors and they'd given it right back to her, untouched. Her problem, and her question, remained: Why do I have to die?

Mylia was behind the church now. She sticks her hand into her bag and takes something out, something small, trailing dust: a piece of white chalk. Chalk to write on her slate. She had forgotten it was in her purse. That morning she'd drawn a house on the slate she kept in her living room. She drew the house where she would live if she didn't die in the meantime. For Mylia, living past the coming months would be like finding out she would live forever. If I don't die, she said, I'll become immortal. Immortal for two years at the most.

She held the chalk. She liked to draw with it. My crude drawings, she called them.

With the chalk in her right hand, she approached the rear of the church. By night, the wall looked yellow, but Mylia couldn't be sure. Nighttime distorts colors, when it doesn't eliminate them completely. Luckily, her piece of chalk was white, obscenely white; she knew it and smiled.

She wrote on the wall, quickly, without giving herself time to think, making letters so small they were barely visible; she wrote: *hunger*.

5

Mylia looked at the rest of the wall and thought: What else should I write on the back of a church at five in the morning?

She tried to remember quotations from the books she'd read that might be right for this particular moment and this particular wall.

But: she felt her stomach throbbing again—with the second, new pain. She lowered her hand, dropping the chalk, and started walking, heading for another street. She was hungry. The pain was becoming unbearable.

Hurrying along, she remembered, almost amused, that the pain of hunger was the pain of life. I'm so hungry, I'm not going to die! It's impossible to die when you're this hungry!

The hunger made her feel strangely safe: the pain of hunger was a guarantee, a promise, at least for the time being. The other pain can't sneak up and kill me when *this* pain is so strong! And now that she felt safe, she tried to take her mind off eating. If I eat something, the hunger pain will pass, and then I'll feel the other pain again . . . and that one *can* kill me.

There was a light in the distance now, maybe a café that was already open, with a telephone booth to its right. The hunger pain was worse and worse. I need to eat something soon or I'll die, she told herself—then laughed at this latest contradiction. She took out a few coins in the booth and put one in the slot, dialed a number and heard it start to ring. No one answered. Four, five, six, seven, eight, nine, ten, eleven, twelve, thirteen, fourteen. Then someone picked up. Ernst, Mylia said, I'm near the church. Hello?

Then she passed out.

Chapter II
Theodor

1

Theodor had just opened a magazine whose centerfold showed a woman with blood pouring out of her nose; she was naked, naked lying on a bed, legs spread wide, ostentatiously displaying her vagina. Another page had this same woman's face with even more blood pouring out. On a third, the woman, now dressed, was opening her mouth wide, in close-up. Way in the back of her mouth, you could see some black teeth.

Theodor went back two pages. He looked at the centerfold again, with the woman on the bed, showing her vagina. Her matted pubic hair looked like a stain—a dangerous, frightening stain. He said something to himself and laughed a little.

He got up and went to the window. The streetlights, positioned every few meters, barely disturbed the dark of night. Large quantities of light are effective in warding off crime—crime and fear; and yet, seen analytically, light is nothing more than a fact of science, Theodor thought.

He was feeling simultaneously aroused and nostalgic that night. A peculiar emotional cocktail, he told himself, with a certain satisfaction.

As he watched, the window—standing between the night and himself—fogged up with his own contradictions. Some force was pulling him out, toward the other side of the glass, demanding that he go downstairs, that he head out in search of human company, pubic hair, pubic *compensation*, he told himself with a perverse smile. The world owes me something for every bad day it's given me.

And yet—at the same time, having looked at those pictures of that woman with her sex on display, Theodor found he couldn't quite shake a certain nostalgic echo. Soon he wouldn't be able to see the nighttime city through his window—there wouldn't be anything there but the face of Theodor Busbeck: doctor, researcher, reputation in decline, ex-husband of Mylia Busbeck.

2

Working as a gravedigger means seeing your own future. Plus, there's something inherently suspicious about a job where doing a little overtime is indistinguishable from committing a crime. Still, to be digging at three in the morning—there had to be something extraordinary going on, Theodor thought, amazed to see so much activity.

"What are you people doing? Chewing on corpses?"

There were two men wearing the same uniform—and uniformity makes you think of order, not crime. Shovels in hand. Gloves. The men looked up and out, in his direction.

"I'm a doctor," he introduced himself. "Dr. Theodor Busbeck."

One of the men greeted him, raised his hand, gave his name, but Theodor couldn't understand him. The other one also introduced himself:

"Kruch. We work here," he said.

"I can see that," Theodor said. "Two men with shovels in their hands must be working."

"We deal with the night dead, Doctor," said the one who had introduced himself as Kruch.

"A recent innovation."

"I'm sorry, Doctor," Kruch said, changing his tone, "but you can't be here."

Theodor looked at the man who had introduced himself as Kruch, then at the other man, who regarded him with an air of indifference. They hadn't moved their shovels since Theodor had arrived. It was impossible to see what they were doing.

"If you ever need me," Theodor said, leaving, "I really am a doctor."

"Sure—we'll give you a call when we're at death's door," Kruch said dryly.

Theodor Busbeck walked away.

The joints of his knees hurt. *The temperature at night makes your bones expand,* Theodor reminded himself, managing to combine his scientific and superstitious tendencies into a single thought. Two hundred meters on, with the cemetery gate a good distance behind him, he stopped and bent his right leg, then his left. The joints of his knees went on hurting.

He repeated the procedure: bending one leg, then the other. Then he continued toward the center of town.

After a brief conversation with two macabre gravediggers, Theodor was thinking, *we now direct ourselves to a brothel. The cemetery was therapy for my nostalgia; now it's time to treat my penis*—speaking this last word out loud, as though he had to explain his methodology, or simply needed to get rid of what little modesty he had left.

Chapter III
Hanna, Theodor, Mylia

1

Hanna had already spent several minutes scrutinizing her eyelids. The mirror was too high; it forced her to stand on tiptoe; she could hardly even see her lips. But: right then, she was working on her lids, touching them up in a shade of purple.

Hanna's fingers gripped a tiny instrument, so to speak—a precision instrument with a long and distinguished history. Purple pencil at work, she was as focused as a surgeon, her right hand steady and determined. The color she was applying, however—microscopically precise—wasn't merely aimed at creating a state of static, perfunctory prettiness; no, Hanna's purple had no interest in being admired . . . it wanted to arouse. Hers would be a utilitarian beauty—not just something for spectators: a resolute beauty, a call to arms. Hanna wasn't purpling her eyelids in order to find love; those eyelids were meant to inspire a man to take a brief (but delightful) vacation from his habitual loneliness. Hanna put more faith in those purple lids—in concert with one of her meaningful looks—than in her short skirt and low-cut shirt; purple eyelids were the key to getting the next guy turned on, the man she'd need to get through another night, she was sure of that. And, when it came to Hanna, *meaningful look* wasn't

GONÇALO M. TAVARES

just an expression. As prostitutes go, she was a unique personality: her *look* was her secret weapon, the most exciting thing about her, really—a combination of depthless perversion and simple, lucid intelligence. It was the look of someone *removed*, an observer, someone experimenting with you—the look of a scientist. Her look even managed to be remote from her own body: she felt like she was watching herself from the outside whenever a man gave her money, whenever the desk clerk handed over the key to their room . . . a room whose romantic modifications ensured that the neighbors had never once been disturbed by the innumerable fornications that occurred there. (Even so, it smelled awful.)

Hanna lowered herself back down onto the pads of her feet, turning away from her mirror. She put away her aesthetic scalpel and picked up her little black bag. She lived in a ground-floor apartment on Georg-Lenz Street with six other women.

"I'm going out," she always tells them. "It's three in the morning—if I don't come back before six, it's because someone's killed me." Then, with a laugh, she slams the door.

2

While he walked by the light of the streetlamps, Theodor Busbeck couldn't help but think about Mylia, his ex-wife. She was eighteen years old when they first met. Theodor, no longer young, was already a doctor then. Mylia's parents had brought her into his office.

"Our daughter isn't healthy," were the first words he heard about his one and only wife.

3

"She isn't healthy? Says who?"

"She never was. Ever since she was a little girl. She has visions . . . that's what she calls them, anyway."

"Visions."

"She sees things. She says she sees things."

"No one can see what another person sees," said Theodor. "We have to rely on them to tell us."

"She says she can see our souls . . ."

"Excellent!" the doctor exclaimed. "That's quite a talent. We doctors still have to use all sorts of machines to look inside people, and we only get pictures of their kidneys and whatnot—nothing at all meaningful. If your daughter can see down into our souls, she's doing considerably better than the medical profession. That's what we call fantastic eyesight!"

But Theodor was the only one who laughed.

"Tell her to come in," he said after a pause. "Let's figure out what's what."

So she came in. Eighteen years old. Discomfitingly, almost violently, beautiful. Nervous Theodor immediately began flipping through some papers on his desk.

"Sit down," he said. "My name is Theodor Busbeck. This is my office. Your parents are about to leave. A doctor should see his patients alone."

Chapter IV
Theodor, Hanna, Mylia

1

Theodor held his breath for a few seconds, then blew warm air onto his hands. The streets were deserted. He was still a few blocks from the center of town, but he could already sense, could already *smell* a little humanity, the spirit of humanity, could already hear movement nearby—distant sounds, cutting through the endless stillness, populating it. Somewhere, human beings were already starting to enjoy themselves.

The next century will have to be a pretty serious one. Otherwise we'll lose everything we've achieved. If we keep wasting our creative energy on useless pastimes, on prostitutes and gossip, another kind of animal will arise—circumspect, humorless—and take over. The simple need to be entertained can bring a whole city down, thought Theodor—perhaps less than sincere. An animal that knew how to distance itself from empty pleasures would have a great biological advantage over human beings . . . and now Theodor couldn't help but think about his own situation: an important doctor, greatly admired for his research—at least he was around three or four years ago—who, at this very moment, at three-something in the morning, was walking the streets, heading for the center of town with a hard-on, unable to get that photo out of his mind, the one he saw just a little while earlier of that woman lying on a bed, blood coming out of her nose and her legs ostentatiously spread, her vagina surrounded by her matted pubic hair; so, important or no, Theodor Busbeck was walking on, determined, steering himself toward a state of absolute uselessness, toward a complete waste of his time, yet an exciting time nonetheless, yes, a time of pure excitement, of enjoyment, and thus efficient in its own way: a *negative* efficiency, a leave of absence from his humanity, a time in which nothing at all is made. If this was all we were—what I am at this moment, rushing through town with a stiff penis, hoping to find a woman as quickly as possible—if this is all we were, we would be no better than our dogs' dogs.

No better than our dogs' dogs, he repeated, and then he saw a whore approaching from the distance, decked out in a short skirt and plunging neckline, her steps just as determined as his—which was strange—her steps mirroring his own. It was Hanna.

2

At eighteen, Mylia already knew how to humiliate men. She understood the liminal space between seduction and repulsion, and she knew how to manipulate that space: shrinking it, expanding it, pretending it didn't exist—just to show off her power. You can only really humiliate the ones you let get close to you . . . she knew that instinctively, getting ready to exercise her perverse talents—first drawing him in, later pushing him away—on that doctor, already eyeing her up and down within minutes of her parents leaving the room . . . leaving the room so that he could do what she'd been hoping for and fearing: interrogate her.

"I'm schizophrenic," she said before Dr. Theodor Busbeck could open his mouth. "I've read books about it. I know exactly what I am. I'm schizophrenic, crazy. I see things that aren't there and I'm dangerous. Do you want to cure me?"

3

"Hello," Theodor said.

The prostitute stopped.

"Now's no good," she said. "I'll be at the center of town in an hour. My name's Hanna. You'll see that it's worth the wait. I'll be on Klirk Purch Street. Go there—I'll be waiting for you."

And Hanna walked away, speeding up again. Theodor stood watching her.

He liked everything about her: her eyes, the arrogant way she spoke, her name, her saying she would be waiting for him, the name of the street where they would meet an hour from now, everything; but mainly the speed with which the encounter had taken place, the efficiency of her words and movements. Theodor had been completely seduced in a matter of seconds. And he knew where to find her again. Efficient as an operating theater, he told himself. An hour from now on Klirk Purch Street.

4

"I'm schizophrenic," Mylia repeated that first day she met her future husband, Dr. Theodor Busbeck. "Schizophrenic."

"You're not a doctor," Theodor said.

"My own mother calls me crazy. You think you know more about me than the people I live with?"

"We should run some tests."

"You can start asking questions," she said.

"Not just questions, medical tests."

"No—only questions."

"Questions aren't proper tests. Anyone can ask questions," Theodor said.

"So ask the right questions."

"And what are those?"

"For instance, if I've ever slept with a man."

"And have you?"

"No."

"All right. So I've asked you a good question, a right question, a question that you asked me to ask. Now can I ask my own questions?"

"No."

"What's your full name?"

"Mylia. I don't want any other names. One is enough."

"Mylia—that's very pretty."

"All the doctors who ask me my name say that it's a pretty name."

"That means it must be true."

"That means it's a lie."

"Mylia is a pretty name, and you're a pretty girl."

"Go to hell."

"Can I ask you another question now?"

"Go ahead."

"Your parents."

"Yes?"

"Do you like them?"

"My mother calls me crazy, but she's right. I threw a glass at her face once. She still has the scars. Did you see them?"

"I didn't notice."

"Well she has them. I'm not making it up. Do you want me to ask her to come back in?"

"No. Answer the question," Theodor said.

"Go to hell."

"Your parents told me that you're able to see our souls."

"It's true."

"What's a soul like?"

"It has pubic hair."

"You're kidding."

"Yes."

"Do you believe in God?"

"I believe in everything they taught me before I turned six. When I was six, I knew more Bible stories than fairy tales."

"So you believe in God."

"I believe in everything they taught me before I turned six. After that, everything they told me was a lie."

"I sympathize with you, Mylia. I hope we can talk again."

"Go to hell."

5

Theodor Busbeck was at the library searching for documents concerning concentration camps, their methods, their locations in different countries and eras—when that girl Mylia sat down next to him and right away noticed the horrific photographs he was looking at. She didn't say anything; she might even have begun to whistle a little tune to herself. She was running the index finger of her right hand over a small imperfection in the table's wood. *A tremendous imperfection*, she thought.

She spent her days contemplating the substance of things. She found materials persuasive. Wood, for instance. The many types of stone and fabrics. Sponges.

She had already figured certain things out concerning the material world. For instance: she was only eighteen years old, and they called her crazy, but despite this—and despite her own certainty that she would never be capable of making any great discoveries—Mylia was certain that all substances in the world have their own velocity, that they move at different rates, very very fast or slow, and that it was this index of velocity that differentiated them.

An egg, any egg, was, for Mylia, a highly disturbing object. It changed so quickly—and, worse, the whole point of its existence was to become something else. Eggs, all eggs, contained a kind of concrete, material altruism that Mylia couldn't find in anything else in the world. Eggs appear because they want to disappear. They appear because they wants to reappear as something else. This material altruism was a moral altruism—and, having found a material altruism, no other seemed worth the name. The spirit isn't generous. The immaterial isn't generous. What does something that doesn't exist have to lose?

Theodor Busbeck liked having Mylia next to him. When she sulked, she was like a plant: rooted to a given place by chance, but likewise seeming to have chosen its location after careful consideration—she distanced herself from Theodor, but not at the opposite end of the room; for Mylia, distancing herself from Theodor meant avoiding physical contact with him, simply not feeling his warmth. One chair away was enough.

She made certain associations. For instance: picking potatoes once, she'd noticed an unusual warmth to them as they came out of the soil, a warmth that surprised her, *a mammalian warmth,* she told herself. So, it was this mammalian warmth, the warmth of an animal able to take up a weapon in order to defend its young and its home . . . this was the warmth that she sensed—as she had in those potatoes—in Theodor Busbeck.

Mylia was only pretending to sulk. She was too curious not to take another look at those awful photographs.

"It's a concentration camp," Theodor said. "Do you know what that is?"

She smiled.

She had been taught two things: seeing and hearing. On her own, she had taught herself—or perhaps her illness had taught her—how to touch. But then, again and again, they told her: *Don't touch people like that.* And she got scared. You aren't supposed to touch people that way? She didn't do it again.

Mylia leaned into Theodor's warmth as she rarely did with her mother. In her solitude, she'd taught herself to touch material things only—things that didn't speak. The way she touched them bordered on the obscene . . . if you can call the encounter, for example, of a human hand and a table—or, specifically, with an imperfection in the wood of a table—obscene.

And still, her mother would say to her, "It's not right to touch things that way."

"So how should I touch them?"

"Use less pressure. Don't grab. Don't get so involved."

What her mother didn't tell her—though other people did—was that she was always reaching out for things as though caressing a lover, as though everything in the world turned her on. So, "It's not right to touch things that way" was, more than anything, a call for modesty.

6

Theodor Busbeck kept thumbing through his book, in which there were several photographs of corpses lying one on top of another on a stairway: small bodies, large bodies, naked, men and women joined together in a parody of pornography, a parody of obscenity; or, rather, embodying another sort of obscenity, see it nestled in between those bodies, one on top of the other—an inverse obscenity, the opposite of the kind that exists between living, healthy things: the obscenity of stasis, without pleasure, without excitement, the obscenity of bodies that would never be desired again, bodies with nothing to offer but horror—an endless, material, indifferent kind of horror—as though to trick you into thinking you aren't looking at people at all, not at men, women, and children reduced to lifeless skin and bone, but at something else, something homogenous, inanimate, a material, a substance: not even something dead, not even the remains of human beings who had once been alive and full of friendly or antagonistic energy—no, merely bodies, bodies that now seemed as though they'd never even been alive: members of an entirely different species, a species that had experienced such enormous obscenity that it had been definitively removed from the core family of *Homo sapiens*, as represented here in the library by one of its exemplary units: a doctor. And his profession makes this moment particularly fascinating: a man tasked with saving bodies, preventing minor illnesses from spreading and major illnesses from running their course, this man, this doctor, Theodor Busbeck, sitting up straight in his chair—in the posture dictated by hygiene and ergonomics—looking on, and on, in horror (yes, there's horror in those brown eyes) at photographs of bodies that are beyond saving, that are beyond the reach of his tools and techniques . . . and, most importantly, his enthusiasm. Indeed, he seems to lack any sort of human response to the photos, aside from repulsion . . . he isn't even able to force himself into a sort of makeshift human response, turning page after page, seeing photograph after photograph, the horror mounting and mounting until it's lost its impact, intensity, awfulness.

"There are more than a thousand bodies in this picture," Theodor said to himself.

It was in the caption: a panoramic shot, a photograph that really got it right—photographs are about getting things right—given the vast scene it was meant to capture . . . how big was the space depicted here, Theodor wondered, in square meters I mean . . . more than forty, less, what? One thing was certain: the caption made explicit a number that the naked eye would have been able to estimate on its own, in a non-numerical, non-scientific, non-measurable way—but a printed *1,000* is far more effective in summing up the utter horror of the photo. One thousand bodies fit into this photograph. One thousand bodies that never even made it to a concentration camp—they died of hunger first. And while Theodor went on sitting there with his eyes fixed on the photograph into which a thousand bodies fit, Mylia, that girl who, at their first meeting, had said: I'm schizophrenic, do you want to cure me?—that girl, right there next to him, not too close and not too far, not too sulky and not too eager, that girl, Mylia, wasn't paying the slightest attention to the horrific photograph; she was looking at the ceiling.

7

Less than two years after their initial—let's call it "professional"—meeting, in which Theodor played the role of the doctor who asks questions and Mylia that of the patient who responds and gets offended, their wedding took place, surprising Mylia's parents and Theodor Busbeck's friends and family.

Though it was obvious that Mylia was going to be trouble.

"You're going to marry a schizophrenic? Good work!" Mylia herself had told Theodor.

Theodor kept trying to convince her that she was wrong.

"I'm the doctor here. I'm the one who decides whether people are sick or well. In some extreme cases I'm even the one who decides whether someone is alive or dead. I'm the one who studied for years, reading books, working with professors—so I'm the one who can tell the difference between a healthy mind and a sick one. I'm the one who gets to say if a woman is healthy or not."

"Do you mean to say," Mylia asked, "that for all those years, long before meeting me, before even knowing I existed, you were already studying my mind, the mind of Mylia? Tell me, which book did you find me in? Which pages was I on? Was the chapter called 'Mylia's

Illness,' or was it—since you seem so convinced—'Mylia's Health'? It's great that someone knows so much about my head! Even I don't know how the thing works, medically. All I know is what it's capable of in extreme situations. My dear husband-to-be, I have nothing but respect for all your years of studying, believe me—your professors, your instruments, your techniques, your books, your pages and pages of diagnoses and treatments, I respect all of that, but, honestly, you need to be more than just a doctor to understand another person's mind . . . you need to be a saint or a prophet, I think. You have to be able to see what's hidden as well as what's right in front of you. And my future husband is a doctor, not a prophet or a saint. Just a doctor."

"I'm going to do a study, recording dates and statistics, comparing the numbers from various sources."

Mylia asked again what the point was, why go back to those books with the horrible pictures. "If you spend all day looking at dead bodies, you'll get used to giving up on people. Doctors shouldn't be fatalists."

"That's ridiculous!" Theodor said.

"So what are you doing it for?" Mylia insisted.

"To understand. I still don't get it."

"I want to produce a graph—a single graph to establish, to summarize, the relationship between history and atrocity. To chart whether horror has been increasing or decreasing century after century. Or else, to find out if there's been a constant amount throughout recorded time. Even if I only discovered a certain historical stability in the level of horror over, say, five centuries, if I was able to demonstrate some kind of regularity, I would already have made a major discovery. I want to develop a graph of everything that's happened up until the present day—since we have more or less reliable historic documents at hand—in the various concentration or death camps. Not in wars—that's beyond my intended scope. I'm not interested in battles between armies, no matter how significant the casualties. War isn't a pure sort of horror. I only want to study situations in which one side has absolutely no ability—or even will—to inflict casualties on the other, and in which the strong side, without any justification whatsoever, decimated the weaker.

"My horror-graph could then lead us to discover something even more basic to the problem of human atrocity: the underlying formula. I mean a numerical, objective, specifically *human* formula—removed from our animal natures, aside from sentiment and instinct, changes of heart, fluctuations in mood—a purely mathematical, purely quantitative, I would even say *detached* formula, implied by my results. But: not merely a formula serving as a concise summary of the *effects* of past horrors; no, my intention is to arrive at another, greater equation; a formula that will allow us to *predict* the horrors to come, that allows us to *act* and not just ponder or lament. I intend to develop a formula laying bare the cause of all the evil men do for no good reason—not even out of fear—the evil that seems almost inhuman, precisely because it's inexplicable. I believe that this is not only possible, but practical. I'm a doctor, a man of science, well trained—not given to flights of fancy. I believe in research, study, analysis. I believe in cautious estimates leading to other cautious estimates; I believe in progression; I respect process; I believe in taking things slow. Research isn't about discovering some hidden treasure lying in wait for us; it's not about wanting something today and expecting to have it tomorrow. It's not about invention or a discovery—it's a form of reasoning, a dialectic, something that's going to take me years and years, maybe my entire life, and maybe my entire life won't even be enough, and someone else will have to continue my work, picking up where I left off. Proper research brooks no gaps: above all, no gaps; it must be one continuous, consistent line; and it's not about poetry, Mylia, it's not about painting a picture, it's much more important, much deeper, an effort that could last centuries; or else, yes, you could say it's *like* painting a picture, but a picture that only grows incrementally, day after day and year after year, a painting that one generation starts and the next will continue, trying to perfect its colors, the light and shadows in it—a painting, if you will, a portrait, but a *historical* portrait, a portrait of how we human beings don't belong to our houses, our parents, our husbands and wives, but instead, and above all, to *History*, to the history of our forebears, to the history of the world. And within that history, a subsection: The History of Horror.

"Mylia, it's important that we understand this. How were all these atrocities committed so fearlessly?

"And I'll arrive at my conclusion in due time, without hurrying, without shouting, without any unnecessary sentimentality; I'll arrive at it rationally, through careful consideration, through logic, methodically. There will be nothing creative, spontaneous, or improvised about my work. I'm a doctor—I have the tools, I learned how to think in a certain way, and I have a plan, as I've already told you: first, I have to gather all possible documents on my subject in order to develop my graph demonstrating the distribution of horror over the centuries; I don't know what the results will be, but somehow I'm fairly certain that I'll end up seeing a consistent pattern spread out in curves like an electrocardiogram, that's right, like the beating of a healthy person's heart, and it's exactly that distribution curve that I'm looking for, the predictable pattern of history's heart, running alongside all the beating of all the hearts of the men who lived it, both of their cardiograms showing their own peaks and valleys, but above all: repetition, predictability, regularity; the history of horror and then the determining substance of history—and every history must have its median, nothing exists without a median. Just like you can see a man's sickness or health spelled out on the graph paper of an electrocardiogram, I intend to be able to see the health or sickness not of a single individual, but of all humanity, in its totality; the health of a collective, of the whole, of all the most relevant, and therefore abject, human behavior. With that graph in hand, I will finally understand what so many before me have sought to comprehend: whether history is sick or healthy, whether history is on the right path or the wrong path, whether there's been any progress over its clinical history, or if, on the contrary, the state of the world is worsening, degrading, developing new infections, new weaknesses; that is, whether history is dying or not . . . whether we're on the verge of a new beginning, of a second history, at the beginning of a second electrocardiogram in human history.

"Like a father who dies and leaves his children a small inheritance—whatever he didn't manage to waste while he was alive—I feel secure in the faith that our first history will bequeath *something* beneficial to the second. What worries me, in the meantime, what unnerves me about my study, and far more than the likelihood of seeing that the prognosis for history is bleak, that its infections are worsening day by day or century by century . . . what frightens me most isn't the prospect of arriving at results demonstrating that the peaks in the horror/time relationship are increasing; no, if our best hope is, finally, to see that horror has been gradually diminishing over time, in a coherent, foreseeable manner, such that we could, for example, predict that it will have ended, definitively, by the year 6000—if this is our best hope, then my greatest fear isn't that the end of horror might mean the end of history, like the flatline of a man who's just died, but rather that the graph doesn't run to either of these extremes, but instead shows nothing but stasis, a terrifying *consistency* of horror over time, a sustained continuo of atrocity that leaves us no hope whatsoever. For instance: a curve discovered in the first three centuries AD repeating itself every three centuries. It's this possibility of eternal return, this tedium, that scares me most. If horror is on the decline, at least our descendents will be a little happier a hundred generations from now . . . and if it's on the rise, history will end in any case, since the ultimate horror won't leave anything behind—and a better, more ethical history might arrive to pick up the pieces. Either of these hypotheses are, in essence, optimistic. But if horror is a constant . . . there's no hope. None at all. Nothing will ever change."

Chapter V
Ernst, Mylia

1

Ernst closed his attic window. He went out and started down the stairs. It had been Mylia's voice on the telephone. And then she'd stopped talking. Something had happened.

He was already on the street. It was about four, maybe five in the morning, dark everywhere. Ernst started to run.

As he ran, he called Mylia's name.

His movements were wholly uncoordinated—his was a bizarre, inefficient method of "running." If he hadn't been an adult male, someone deserving of respect—anyway, whatever respect is due a forty-year-old, or someone in the neighborhood of forty—one might be tempted to say that he didn't *know how* to run. When his right leg moved forward, it took a detour to the side, thus setting his entire body off balance—which he then made up for, instinctively, by thrusting his torso so far forward that it looked like he'd have to fall flat on his face. But Ernst's body had been conditioned to accommodate these constant disturbances: it always recovered, seemingly at the last minute, with a new forward movement of the right leg, a movement likewise accompanied by an unnecessary detour to the side.

Still. However he did it, Ernst ran. And since it was nighttime, no one really noticed his fitful and erratic progress.

The streets were still practically empty. Streetlights escorted his lopsided steps down the sidewalk.

Ernst had run straight toward the church nearest his house, following a street only a few blocks from the center of town.

A few more paces and he saw a heap of something lying next to a telephone booth. He nearly tripped over himself in his excitement—his disobedient right leg kicked out a little too forcefully—but he made it to the something, which had feet, and a head. He reached out to it. It was Mylia.

1

Theodor and Mylia Busbeck's first years together weren't easy. It had nothing to do with the age difference between them—close to ten years. The problem was more what you could call a *health difference.* As a doctor, Theodor wasn't just healthy himself (how robust he was, how lively!), he demanded that everyone around him be healthy too—more than a professional obligation, it was a vendetta: he practically *ordered* his patients to be healthy; he shoved health down their throats, as it were, via medication, operations, etc. He wanted—he needed—to be surrounded by health, to have it propping him up, *existentially.*

His energy seemed inexhaustible. He worked at a state clinic for part of the day, and in the afternoons went to the main library to do research for his project—still trying to understand horror and history, and, through them, mankind. Health was so paramount to him that he needed to understand the concept in broader terms, not just one patient at a time: the mental health of a city, for instance, seen as an organized and efficient unit tasked with the suppression of violence. His ultimate goal was to gauge the sanity of history itself.

Thus, his life was split between the clinic and the library: doing practical and immediate work in the mornings, trying to heal whomever happened to be assigned to him (or at least improve their chances of survival)—wrestling with the particulars of a life, a tangible and individual human being—and then, in the afternoons, devoting himself to the ephemeral, to work that had no visible effects on his daily life or anyone else's, and that, in a way, took him away not only from his morning, but from his entire century, thereby satisfying another of his basic needs: to feel like he was being useful to future generations. As a doctor, he could save individuals from his *own* generation, of course, the ones he actually crossed paths with, but through his utopian project, trying to understand the workings of history, Theodor hoped to do more—and it was a matter, he said, of excising death and suffering from the world, not just increasing comfort, as the inventors of certain machines had done; that is, he yearned to be able to save people he'd never even meet, as though he didn't want to be a doctor after all, but, really, a saint, just like Mylia had said: a saint not only capable of understanding his wife's mind, not only capable of understanding the mind of his fellow man—or even of all men, in their totality—but a perfect saint of the intellect, capable of seeing down into the marrow of history, capable of understanding Its thoughts . . . or at least of graphing out the *way* It thought. If he could manage it—if he could treat history like an organism with a consciousness, with a brain—and if through documentation and research he arrived at his graphs and formulas, and they actually did explain the nightmare of the past twenty centuries, Theodor would have achieved what thousands of men—famous and obscure, violent and peaceful—had tried before him: he would have mastered history. So he went from small to great, particular to general, morning to afternoon, relying on his experiences as a doctor treating the mentally ill: he knew that the best way to understand the way such people thought was to force them to adopt a regular routine: once you can predict how a person will act, you've begun to control him. His methods as far as history were more or less the same: he would study it until he began to see Its patterns. Then, he would control it.

And yet. Theodor found himself afraid of the thing that most excited him. How could he live with himself if he were to succeed? If he actually managed to reach a point in his work where he could understand the rationale behind a concentration camp, the extermination of thousands of men and women, young and old—and therefore consider it perfectly normal? He feared his uncommon ability—so often praised—to understand the mentally ill. That knack of *getting inside a stranger's head*, as some of his colleagues had put it—his way of empathizing with the pathological—could breed something . . . improper. If he learned to understand the pathology of history . . . if he were able to get inside Horror's head and engage it in a rational conversation . . . what would follow?

2

Despite this fear of his own mind and where it might be leading him, Theodor was, by any standard, the picture of health: physically, mentally, spiritually. In fact, these three categories represented the essential axis around which all of Theodor's life—or at least his sense of his own life as being a healthy one—revolved. In this regard, seeing health as a *holistic process*, he was rather more open-minded than the majority of his colleagues at the clinic, who tended to boil down mental health to *a state in which our muscles always do what we want and we always want them to do something sensible*. To Theodor, that kind of "healthy" person—with "normal" desires and the "normal" muscles to carry them out—was still missing what he called *spiritual normality*. And what does spiritual normality entail? Here's Dr. Busbeck's theory: The truly healthy man necessarily spends most of his life trying, like a child, to find what he feels he's missing . . . because he lives with a feeling of constant *loss*, and this sensation is easily mistaken for the feeling of *having been robbed*, the feeling that someone has stolen something very important from you, *a part of your own self*—a part that, for the sake of argument, we'll agree to call "spiritual." So: the truly healthy man, wanting to become whole, goes off in search of the burglars and whatever it was they took—even though he couldn't really tell you what he's missing, doesn't know the shape or substance of his stolen goods. It was the initial discovery, the realization that one has been robbed—on a spiritual level—that Theodor saw as the essential thing. A truly healthy man wants to find God—to put it more directly. And Theodor didn't just say this in private conversations with his colleagues—he mentioned God at conferences too; something that left many doctors in his field perplexed, almost outraged, feeling that the mention of God in a professional, medical context was akin to heresy. Nonetheless, Theodor held fast to his opinions—or his instincts, as he put it—legitimizing them, provocatively, by referring to them as *scientific*.

What conclusion, finally, did the *scientific instincts* of Theodor Busbeck—and of which he was so proud—lead him to develop? We could sum it up as follows: A man who doesn't seek God is crazy . . . and crazy people need to get treatment.

3

But, as we were saying . . . Theodor and Mylia Busbeck's first years together weren't easy.

In terms of the triad of categories essential to every healthy person—according to Theodor—Mylia was in fine fettle on the physical and spiritual fronts: she had an efficient body that obeyed her in every possible way (inasmuch as standard human anatomy allows), and that efficient body of hers was certainly seeking God, certainly feeling that something was missing, something she knew could never be found in the material world. The one category where Mylia was deficient—and Theodor, canny as he was, had understood this the very first time they'd spoken . . . the moment he'd fallen in love with the girl who announced that she was schizophrenic and then started insulting him—was *mentally*, in her desires. She was sick in the head, as the neighborhood kids said—sometimes out loud, cruelly, so she could hear them.

As such, Theodor had hardly been expecting an easy transition to married life. He understood her mind; in a way, he'd already begun to regulate it; he was able to predict her reactions with only a tiny margin of error—her brutal tantrums, increasingly offensive insults, and all

Mylia's other utterly illogical behavior . . . inexplicable, inconvenient, and impossible. So it would be misleading, really, to say that their difficulties were due to Mylia's illness. No, their problems were the same problems that every man and woman have when they're learning to live together, since both Mylia and Theodor—like the rest of us—had what we tend to refer to as *personalities*. Mylia's perhaps was a little peculiar, but Theodor already understood it, knew how to adapt himself to her; like Mylia was trying to do for him, since—naturally—just because her husband was such a robust and lively man didn't mean he was a tabula rasa: Theodor too was an individual—unique, alone, separate from other living beings—and had his own personality, difficult or not, calling out for understanding.

Our point being, here, that Theodor's therapeutic techniques and quasi-scientific instinct had, from the start, made the couple's relationship basically one of equals, despite his *health* and her *illness*. So please believe that it wasn't out of self-defense, out of anything less than noble—out of *not being able to stand her differences anymore*—but because Mylia was really and truly becoming a danger to herself, that, after several violent episodes, Theodor decided—on the 31st of December to be exact; during the eighth year of their marriage—to commit his wife, Mylia, to the second floor of the Georg Rosenberg Asylum, the best-regarded mental institution in the city.

Chapter VII
Hinnerk, Hanna

1

There were only two things—if you could call them that—that Hinnerk kept from the war: a gun, which he always wore under his shirt, on the inside of his pants; and a constant feeling of fear that—precisely because it never went away—took on a very different place in his life, over the years, as compared to the other more-or-less dramatic crises that interfere, time to time, with our nervous systems. Since it never left, this fear was like a tangible, physical fact for Hinnerk, like a crooked nose, a dead eye, or a limp. Hinnerk never left home without his fear; never stayed in without its keeping him company; never slept alone, since the fear was always with him. Even at moments when he was barely conscious, when he was asleep and dreaming, seemingly relaxed, when the most basic, fragile filaments of his personality were exposed, yes, even *then* there was a kind of bitterness ruling the landscape of seeming chaos behind his eyes—the flickering, uncontrollable images, the fractures in the possible, the alien times and spaces. If humanity is a State, a State of Individuality, a State that reportedly fluctuates while we sleep, oscillating between coherence and dissolution, Hinnerk's never relaxed, never dissolved: it was the only way he could keep safe, and his bitterness—fixed like a stake in his mind—was nothing less than a *military precaution*, if you will: a precaution that was never once allowed to slacken, any more than a drill sergeant might be persuaded to let you take a nap . . . as though even this supposedly private, personal space—sleep—hadn't escaped the strict rule of wartime. As a result, Hinnerk had a terrible time relaxing . . . he woke up most mornings feeling as though he'd just been in a duel to the death.

The defining features of his face were the bags under his eyes, like some nocturnal animal's. They were as noticeable as a wound, blemish, or deformation—and as hard to look at—the skin folding over itself several times. Yes, there was a concentration around his eyes, not just of wrinkled skin, but of intensity too—the rest of Hinnerk's body was amorphous and unremarkable: he *was* those eyes, that skin. And as far as that "landscape" behind them, that miniscule country, the basis for their expression . . . well, various things had happened to Hinnerk, of course, and some—the most intense ones, the ones that changed him—had stuck to the inner border of his eyes like a greasy residue, and that stain, unequivocal as a scar, revealed his bitterness to the world and everyone in it; while the puckered skin, for its part, likewise unequivocal, if a little more mundane, could perhaps be traced back to the bottle a certain person broke in another person's face in the middle of a certain fight . . . a real scar serving as both reminder and exhibit. We could even put a date to it. But let's not chalk up the *gravity* of Hinnerk's eyes to simple facts. There was something more complex going on in and around them—they were a synthesis of all the unpleasant details of his life, transmuted over the years into base matter, *terrified* matter, a physical manifestation of his fear, his fear of other men, of someone—anyone—approaching him . . . and, as such, they themselves were rather alarming. Hinnerk lived in constant fear of his fellow men—and yet, how many times, when he passed them on the street, had people said (and so casually . . . as though reciting their address or giving driving directions): look at that one, *he has the face of a killer.*

Hinnerk lowered his head so he wouldn't hear.

2

By keeping to a predictable and monotonous routine, Hinnerk tried to diminish the incursion of what might be called *novelty* into his life. In peacetime, he'd quickly come to understand that there was a link between fear and the unexpected; thus, he subjected his days to unrelenting surveillance, splitting himself in two—prisoner and warder—so as to keep as close a watch as possible on both the world and himself.

At home, he trained with mannequins. In his soundproof basement, laying his targets down on their sides, hiding them behind old sofas or armoires, leaving only the slightest trace of them visible—a target's foot or one of its hands (which, given this new emphasis, seemingly detached from the rest of its body, seemed as important as any head or heart)—Hinnerk would fire.

There was a school for children between six and ten years old at the other end of his street. Every one of the kids had already run into *The Man with the Face of a Killer*. He'd proved a handy bogeyman: they even threatened each other with him when someone went too far calling names, or when a bigger boy was beating up a smaller ... *I'm going to call Him* was what they'd say—and it got results. Even certain unthinking teachers sometimes threatened to *call The Man* if one of their students refused to settle down.

In the meantime, one of Hinnerk's few pleasures in life was looking through his window and watching the children have fun, so fearless and carefree. From his window, using a set of small binoculars, he kept an eye on the schoolyard, developing the habit of watching the children during their after-lunch recess.

Sometimes, without any intention of firing—the gun wasn't even loaded—Hinnerk picked up his pistol, went to the window and, holding his binoculars in his left hand, pointed the barrel at one of the children; he would follow its movements for a few seconds, finally abandoning the child's haphazard path, lowering his gun and binoculars, and drawing the white curtain. Then he'd get ready to go out.

3

The only woman who ever visited Hinnerk's house was Hanna. Under the circumstances, she was more or less his girlfriend.

Hanna always left some of the money she'd earned the night before—on the streets—*at her boyfriend's house*, but there was nothing you could call an agreement between them, even an unspoken one; there wasn't any real correspondence between what Hanna earned on a given night and the amount she left behind on Hinnerk's living-room table; and she almost always left it without comment, as if out of habit, without a second thought—she took the money out of her purse and dropped it on the table with all the ceremony of tapping ashes into an ashtray; as if, in fact, the money didn't mean a thing to her, wasn't of any importance, was just something left over, like cigarette ashes, a waste product from the night before. The expression *this is what's left over from last night*—which was as close to an acknowledgment of her largess as she ever made—took on a double meaning in this context: the money was indeed a leftover, it wasn't what was important; what was important *to her* was what had taken place over the night in question. Whatever money Hanna earned was secondary—her primary motivation was pleasure. I enjoy myself at night, and this is just what happens to be left over: money.

Nevertheless: it was all the money Hinnerk ever saw. And he never thanked Hanna, not even once—nor was he aware that this might have seemed discourteous. *That*—the money left on the table—was already a fact, a given, a circumstance which, because it was so reliable, because it'd never faltered, had, like his fear, taken root in his anatomy, become a part of him. He always scooped it up with his right hand on his way out the door, crumpling it up and shoving it into his pants pocket like a bunch of scrap paper. He wasn't conscious of it. The money wasn't just his, it was *him*.

Hanna had caught Hinnerk twice now with his gun and his little binoculars—his unsteady hand aiming at a child. One of those times she'd even asked him *if the bullet would make it all the way there.*

We're far away, Hinnerk agreed.

Chapter VIII

Hanna, Hinnerk

1

Hanna was in a hurry the night she ran into Theodor Busbeck because she was on her way to Hinnerk's house. She was worried.

Hinnerk had seemed more violent than usual the last few days, which meant that his fear was on the rise. Whenever that happened, he wouldn't even leave the house—he'd just spend his days practicing his aim, as if there really were some kind of threat . . . He needed to be ready.

This time, though, something in particular was bothering him. He'd noticed that the local children had stopped giving him so wide a berth. This meant that they'd become less fearful—less fearful of *Him*. A few times now, when he'd been passing some of them in the street, Hinnerk had distinctly heard one child or another say: hey look, *here comes The Man*.

And this little phrase had gradually turned into a kind of taunt, at once secret and obscene: *here comes The Man*.

Sometimes, after passing a group of children, Hinnerk smiled, hearing in that mantra of theirs a kind of childish wonder, as though he was some kind of exemplar of his species: look, here comes *The Man*! Like in a children's show, where all the animal kingdoms are introduced one by one by the announcer: hey everyone, here's the plant, and now here comes the dog, and—careful!—last but not least, here comes the man, *The Man* himself . . . and Hinnerk walks on stage, basking in the children's applause. Here is The Man: he's arrived at last, it's me.

But Hinnerk understood. He felt the children's hostility. *Here comes The Man* also means: *you're not a man at all* . . . and likewise: *I don't ever want to be like that Man.* And Hinnerk laughed, alone, over those insignificant, childish cruelties. He was still a strong man, after all—he'd been to war, he'd fought and killed many enemies, escaped ambushes, ate badly, and braved the cold of night wearing nothing more than a sweater if that's what it took to help a comrade. And he still had a gun, remember, right there under his shirt. How perfectly ridiculous the cruelty of a child is under these circumstances, he thought. At any moment he could take out his gun and shoot one of them dead; it would be easy . . . *child's play.* So why are these kids so stupid? Hinnerk wondered. Why risk so much, despite their fear?

Because he would never do anything like that. He was scared too, always, but he would never show it . . . he wouldn't expose himself to attack like they did. He hid, he didn't make fun of people, he just concentrated on preparing himself, practicing his aim; if it ever became necessary to act, he'd be ready. When they threaten me, I won't jeer at them, I won't raise my voice, *I'm getting ready to respond non-verbally.* Hinnerk had no illusions about being able to rely on legal forms of defense—the Law, the Constitution!—he wasn't a *respectable* person, and he'd been in the war: he knew words were meaningless, *they had no weight*, a single bullet weighs more than ten thousand words. So, really, he felt sorry for those kids . . . just that: sorry. There was a certain dreaminess about them, a *not-being-in-the-world*, a deep distraction . . . the only appropriate response was pity. *They can't even conceive that, from one moment to the next, I could decide to open fire, and their lives would be over . . .*

But they might as well have had their backs to him, hands in the air. What was the point of shooting down a defenseless enemy?

That's what Hinnerk told himself, but even though he knew that their cruelty—to him, to his eyes, to those bags under his eyes (they made fun of them, he knew they did, Hinnerk wasn't blind)—was based on innocence, ignorance, ingenuousness, an enormous *lack of attention*, he'd still become deeply irritated by their mounting courage, and just three days ago now he'd barely been able to restrain himself, at the last minute, from picking one of those little imbeciles up—chanting *here comes The Man!* as loudly as it could—grabbing the kid by its shirt and pulling it right up to his face, bringing the ugly bags under his eyes as close as possible to the child's own, so that the kid would never forget them, yelling all the while: I'm *not* a man, I'm something else, *something else*!

2

So Hanna was worried about Hinnerk, who just yesterday had told her his fear was getting worse; there was no reason for it, but he felt threatened, like something could happen at any moment. They were after him, he said, he hadn't done anything, hadn't committed any crimes; the war had been over for years, and he'd been on the winning side. It had been ages since anyone actually threatened his life, and he had a gun, he wore a gun in peacetime, he practiced his aim every day, he was ready for anything. But still: he was afraid, always afraid, and his fear was growing.

It was a little after three-thirty in the morning when Hanna knocked at his door—Hinnerk had never given her a key. She knocked several times, no one answered. Hinnerk had gone out.

She stood there for a few minutes, leaning against the door. Then: panic.

She started walking, and despite her short, tight skirt, once she was back in the street, she accelerated until she was practically running. She was afraid.

Chapter IX
The Mental Patients

1

Gada is speaking. Fifteen years old.

I'm always going in and out of this place. They open me like a door and then they close me again. They operated on me for eleven years. Seventeen operations. They made me a door for eleven years. They opened me and closed me. They opened me and closed me. And they also made a door in my head.

And Gada, just fifteen years old, has a scar on his head.

I don't have a shadow, says Heinrich.

It's hot. Heinrich, under the shade of a tree, is smoking a cigarette, and when he spits he spits so forcefully that none of his saliva falls inside the shade. I'm having a contest with my spit, he says. To see if my spit can reach farther than the tree's shadow.

He walks away from the tree and goes into the sunlight to recover his own shadow. You see, he points. I'm not dead.

He looks down at his feet and spits at his right.

Madame, I need water, Heinrich says. But there's no Madame around.

She has a fever and wants to break through the glass. I can't feel my hand, Mylia says. If I break the glass with my hand, I'll be able to feel my hand again.

Witold says: And if you can't feel your soul, break the glass with your soul. He laughs.

Souls aren't meant to break glass. Hands are used to it.

I can't feel my hand, Mylia says.

He asks her how many fingers she has. Five fingers.

See, you still have your whole hand.

No, my hand is missing, Mylia says.

Two men grab her. Mylia opens and closes her right hand dozens of times.

I'm going to sweep the hotel, Marksara says.

The hotel is dirty, it has crumbs and men. And cigarette butts.

I'm going to sweep the hotel. It's full of men, Marksara says. And cigarette butts.

The men smoke a lot.

I'm always sweeping, Marksara says.

They locked me up here so my mother wouldn't see me die.

Johana says she understands.

A mother shouldn't see her daughter die.

Johana is cutting the fingers off a glove so she can mend them later with wool thread.

And save the fingers, she says, laughing.

She doesn't have scissors. She tears the fingers off the gloves by grabbing them tight, then ripping them with her teeth.

My mother has strong teeth, Johana says.

They locked me up here so she wouldn't see my teeth. My mother locked me up here.

Marko watches television all day long. From the moment he wakes up until he goes to sleep. No one can pull him away.

Anything could happen, he says.

He has a hat.

He says that the hat affects his mind. But he doesn't want to throw it away.

It causes hysterics, he says about the hat.

My hat isn't heavy, he says, holding it out. You can put it on and you won't topple over.

But no one takes the hat. He puts it back on his head.

It was my father who gave it to me. When I turned fifteen. It's small.

The man lowers his head and begins to cry.

She has a number 53 on her sweater and is eating dessert.

I'm Martha.

And she's very thin.

Martha says: I'm very thin.

She points at the number 53 on her sweater.

I was happy three times.

When my mother let me play in the garden.

Then my mother brought me here. I thought it was a game.

The only landmarks below her collarbone are the bones of her thin legs.

My mother said my clothes didn't have a body in them.

He has various maps in his bag. Maps of the world, of Europe, of Asia.

Stieglitz says: Now we are here.

Whenever he stops walking, he takes the maps out of his bag and looks at them. Then he uses a pointer to indicate his location.

We are here.

He never says: *I* am here. He always says: *We* are here.

Every day, the same routine. The borders of the countries on his maps have been almost entirely effaced by all the scuffing from his pointer.

Whenever he sees someone new, Stieglitz goes up to him and whispers:

Could you give me some maps?

When the someone says he doesn't have any, Stieglitz gets violent.

Then he goes quiet. He looks at the someone and smiles.

I swallowed a nail, I have a nail in my throat.

Wisliz opens his mouth. He points at a small groove.

The nail is here. He points.

The nail won't let me sing.

When I was a boy, I ate snails. I picked them up and ate them. My father didn't like my eating them. He said they brought bad luck.

Rodsa is afraid of suffocating.

I was a very rich woman, she says.

Rodsa is fifty years old.

When they tell her her age, she asks: What's that?

They explain that her age is actually many times greater than the week that's passed since her brother last visited.

Rodsa says: I don't know what fifty years are.

Rodsa is thin and smokes a lot.

The last time my brother visited, Rodsa says, I wore a short dress. So he could see my legs.

My brother brought me cigarettes.

Rodsa touches her crotch three times for luck.

I'm still going to have three sons, she says.

Rodsa slaps her crotch with her right hand three more times.

Rodsa doesn't have any children.

Zero percent doesn't exist, says Uberbein, who was once a mathematician.

His hair fell out because he went to a whore.

I'll stay hairless till summer. That's what they told me.

But zero percent doesn't exist, he repeats.

Uberbein puts his hand in his pocket and brings it out full of salt.

If zero percent existed, this wouldn't be here.

He almost starts to cry. He pulls himself together.

My hair fell out because I went to a whore.

I was a professor of mathematics, Uberbein says.

I'll be bald till summer.

She has short, gray hair.

She could be everyone's mother.

Laras is sixty-five years old.

They say there's something wrong with my head, but it's a lie, Laras says. My mother also had short hair like me—and she died of heart trouble.

They say there's something wrong with my head, but I'm not going to die from head trouble. The trouble is with my heart, not my head.

I'll die when my heart stops.

My mother also had short hair.

Laras points her chin in the air.

See? I could be everyone's mother.

Janika is black and likes to make food.

I like to make food, Janika says.

She puts everything she can find into a pan. Rocks, weeds, cigarette butts, small pieces of paper.

You can't waste anything, she says.

Janika is fifty years old.

I've gone hungry, Janika says. You can't waste anything.

Some men throw their cigarette butts directly into the wastebasket she carries around.

I've gone hungry. I like to make food, Janika says.

Paola is in love.

I met a guy, Paola says, and she starts laughing and lifts up her skirt.

Paola is forty years old and Rudi, the guy, is thirty-two.

I met him here, Paola says.

It was here. Paola points to the hallway leading to their rooms.

Paola says: Rudi's crazy.

I'm going to braid my hair so he'll think I'm pretty.

But he's crazy, he laughs all the time.

I know I shouldn't braid my hair for someone who just laughs all the time. But I also know I'm not pretty, Paola says.

Vana squeezes Markso's genitals through his pants.

He's got a big one, Vana says.

The biggest one here. I've seen them all.

One day they were in the shower, Vana says, and I opened the door and saw them.

Markso's was the biggest one.

Markso is leaning against a tree. He's smoking a cigarette. Every time Vana touches his genitals, he seems distracted for a moment, but he remains indifferent.

All Markso does is smoke.

It's filthy here, Mylia says.

They never wash me.

Mylia is constantly lifting up her skirt. She shows her genitals to everyone.

It's filthy here, Mylia insists. It's filthy, but they put in a garden.

I know it's a disgrace to lift my skirt up, but I've always liked showing people. I used to be clean, but here, it's filthy.

I was brought here. It was my husband, Dr. Busbeck. He's important. He says I see souls.

Mylia points to the garden. It's filthy here. Why do you suppose they bothered putting in a garden? she asks.

They never wash me here, it disgusts them to wash my thing, Mylia says.

Wisliz has a scar on his head.

They operated on my head, Wisliz says.

They took my brains.

They say I'm stupid, that I don't understand.

I'm tired, I can't concentrate.
I need to sleep a lot, says Wisliz.

Ernst. The others all make fun of the way Ernst runs.
My name is Ernst. Ernst Spengler.
I like it here.

Chapter X

Kaas

1

The boy tries to sleep belly down, but can't. He gets up, determined, then stops, sits down. He lets himself collapse back onto the bed again. Unaccustomed to his body after sleep, Kaas Busbeck is reacquainting himself with its solidity . . . and inconvenience. While he was up, he'd seen himself in the mirror.

His legs were too thin. Dangerously so. The army would never take him. And so these first few moments of consciousness—still hazy from his nightmares—were clouded, as ever, by unhappiness. Kaas lit a match. He saw: night. The burning match in his hand was proof that it was still night. Then he looked at his knees. His knees were proof that his legs would never improve. They were, themselves, like matchsticks. Running was completely out of the question. Kaas would never be able to chase after anyone. He would never be able to run away from them either. A congenital, general dystrophy, the doctors had said. Just like that. As though his body was determined to keep him from moving. Was this just laziness on its part, Kaas wondered, or simple logic? *You're already here, and everywhere else is more or less the same—why bother running?*

Theodor Busbeck, his father, had said: Certain handicaps are nature's way of responding to our most secret desires.

Back in bed, Kaas picked up his watch. He pretended it was some terrible peephole. You could look through it and catch time itself at work. He brought his eye up to it, wondering if there might be something else on the other side—something other than the hours and minutes the little machine pretended to count. With his eye against the glass that protected the hands marking out their units of time, Kaas imagined now that the clock's works were a separate and mechanical universe, and that he was a vengeful god above it, a bringer of catastrophe—the unexpected introduction of a single one of his long eyelashes into those hours, minutes, seconds, would be enough to throw the regular order of our days into disarray . . .

But no, he took his eye away, the watch-hands remained intact, protected by a stupid piece of glass. Kaas got out of bed again and opened the door to the hall. A light in the living room, but it was empty. His father's door was closed.

The other kids were different from Kaas. He'd felt alienated as far back as he could remember. And it wasn't just because of his legs—which were, you know, absurdly, monstrously thin, at least in comparison to the rest of his body—or even his peculiar way of walking, with his weight distributed in all the wrong places . . . no, it was also his personal interests that kept him apart, that marked off an unbridgeable gap between Kaas and other boys and girls his age.

He smelled something. He went to the kitchen. Nothing special, just two dirty plates.

More than anything, his speech left him most open to ridicule—more so than his legs. He could stand still, for instance, not walk, or even sit with his legs out of sight if he needed to, but it's difficult to stay quiet in the middle of a group, it just can't be done indefinitely; if you sit with

·

them, this shows a certain submission to the collective, but prolonged silence is a provocation, it demonstrates a minor but indisputable inclination toward revolution—perhaps confined to a single room and half a dozen comrades, perhaps minimal and insignificant, but revolution nonetheless: a will to negate the progress of history. Thus, Kaas had to speak, at least every once in a while, and when he did, his words were out of control: certain of them ending prematurely, involuntarily, while others were delayed until there was no more need for them—as though his sentences were all in a fragile boat being tossed around by a storm. His father, Theodor, would say to him: Hold on to your sentence, hold tight like it's an oar, hold on as hard as you can, don't let it get away from you . . .

But Kaas couldn't manage it.

2

In photographs, he looked perfectly healthy. He was certain, for example, that a distant relative, a Busbeck living on the other side of the planet and who only received news from his father by mail, would have no idea that he wasn't a normal boy. Theodor chose which photographs to send to people and never made any written references to his son's handicaps—thus fueling, albeit without actually lying, the misapprehension the photographs encouraged. In a photo, of course, Kaas's tiny and skeletal legs were easily hidden, and his speech impediment, obviously, was invisible—and in a visual document, the visible is all that matters. For this reason (and perhaps other ones too), Kaas took up an unexpected hobby, which he pursued alongside his studies—and there too he wasn't much of a star, even at his "special" school, only managing to muddle through thanks to enormous effort, and the added support of father's good name, thanks to which he wasn't much more than one year behind the rest of his age group . . . Along with going to school, then, Kaas also took up photography, which gradually came to be his one great enthusiasm—containing as it did elements of all the things in life Kaas actually found somewhat comforting: working with his hands, for instance, he was very good with his hands, even earning some grudging respect on this front among his classmates; and then, keeping quiet for long periods of time—or, perhaps, more to the point: finding himself able to do away with conversation without there being any consequences. Finally, the images that Kaas created—or captured—became a way to exhibit something of himself while staying hidden: a way of being with other people, at least from the waist up: people didn't pity or ridicule him when he was taking pictures; when he was behind a camera, Kaas became a human being who could compete with everyone else, and on the same level: he turned into someone you could have a conversation with.

As for the other parts of his life, well, the thing that had made the most impression on him was an argument he'd been in at school one time; a bout of petty name-calling between himself and a relatively fit classmate had gotten more and more intense until the two boys basically had to start hitting each other or else be shown up as cowards; they'd reached that special point in a confrontation where violent physical contact is not only inevitable but *essential*—when, suddenly, Kaas's opponent had stopped, as though remembering something he'd been trying to call to mind all afternoon. He backed off then, he stepped away, he retreated (in other circumstances he would've been branded a coward for the rest of the year), saying: I can't fight you.

Kaas had as much upper-body strength as any of his classmates. It was his legs that wouldn't cooperate—certainly not when you consider all the exigencies of a playground fight between schoolboys, "special" or otherwise. You'd hardly have to touch his legs and he'd be down—the fight would be over in seconds. So there wasn't any point to Kaas throwing punches . . . he didn't really have any legs.

I can't fight you. That was the most offensive thing Kaas had ever heard.

3

But there was something strange about this particular night's insomnia. Another clock, in the kitchen, brightly displayed the time: three-fifty. But the strangeness had nothing to do with Kaas's simply waking up; he'd already been up several times that night. What was odd was the incredible silence hanging over the house. It was quieter than usual.

He drew aside the curtain and looked out a nearby window at the silent, deserted street. This was only to be expected: the Busbeck residence was in one of the best neighborhoods in town—quite convenient to the central business district—and there was never any activity at that hour. But the problem wasn't outside. The excessive silence that had woken Kaas wasn't coming from the street; it was coming from inside the house.

He left the kitchen and went to his father's room. He leaned his ear against the door: nothing, not a single noise. He worked up the courage to open it. The room was empty. Theodor had gone out.

Kaas stood still for a few seconds, shocked—as though he'd just been given some terrible news, as though he had to take a quick breath before allowing himself to become afraid. But this paralysis didn't last long. He walked back to his room and got dressed. He was going out to search for his father.

More than anything, he was annoyed. As a doctor and a father, Theodor had no right to leave Kaas alone in the middle of the night. It's nothing less than an act of cowardice, he said.

Chapter XI
Hinnerk

1

Hinnerk didn't much care how the war might have traumatized his ex-comrades-in-arms. One day he ran into a member of his platoon; the man had a horrible tic and recognized Hinnerk at once. This veteran squeezed his hand: Hinnerk, Hinnerk Obst! he said. They spoke slowly to one another, choosing subjects that were general enough that they wouldn't be forced to reminisce. They then parted ways and that was that.

In any conversation, Hinnerk always assumed the role of the person trying to cut things short, the one who was in a rush. *I don't have time to play games,* he'd say.

He was firm. He didn't have time to play games. Like he'd thrown all his words into a pit and buried them. Words *annoyed him.* Not just adjectives, but also those nouns, all trying to designate things in the tangible world. Verbs too, of course. I was a soldier, he'd say, when someone pointed out that he wasn't much of a talker.

Hinnerk was measuring his table with a ruler. The proportions of a piece of furniture are important. The table had perfect, fixed dimensions.

Hinnerk wanted to simplify his life, but there was an ink stain on his table, complicating it. How thick the stain was—as though the ink had taken it upon itself to raise the surface of the table. Big brownish dents in the stain proved that someone had tried to scrape the ink away, but had finally given up.

When Hinnerk moved his hand over the table, he could feel the tiny bump of the stain with his fingers. Like a mountain range, it had areas of greater and lesser altitude. If his hand were a traveler, a set of feet following a trail, the stain would be a slope, an obstacle, calling for greater effort, an area requiring *his hand to climb.*

Hinnerk put his gun on the table, next to the stain. A gun doesn't make the same kind of mountain as an ink stain. It's made out of different stuff entirely.

He felt a slight pressure in his neck and brought his left hand up to probe for the source of this discomfort. Yes, he must have gotten it: the pressure subsided.

Now he lowered his head and put his nose up to the gun. The gun had a smell, a particular smell. Not at all like hot food, Hinnerk thought with a smile . . . but it wasn't entirely unpleasant.

He lifted his head and then brought it down again. He smelled the gun again. First with his nose up against the barrel, then against the trigger, then the grip. Each part of the gun had a different smell. If he really concentrated, if he focused exclusively on smelling the gun, he would be able to differentiate the olfactory qualities of every section. Discrete stimuli, hidden by proximity, like the smells of three different foods served on the same plate. Again, Hinnerk smiled.

There would be grounds for saying that Hinnerk had a certain obsession with guns. In this respect, one might assume that the war had

had its compensations for him. But no. He couldn't remember ever looking at guns during the war. As if the *act* of war, which took place through and with and because of guns, had erased the possibility of his *enjoying* them as an enthusiast. Only now, years later, could Hinnerk *see* guns again. As a spectator.

He smelled his way back to the barrel, then over to the grip; and now, in fact, having spent the requisite amount of time with his nose against its metal—feeling the slightly unpleasant heat radiating from the thing—sitting at his table, completely focused, in total silence, with no other thoughts in his head, Hinnerk found he was able to smell his own hands on the gun. The grip of a gun smells like a man—in this case like a man by the name of Hinnerk Obst. The smell of a man is a human smell, he thought, then went back to concentrating and inhaling. What a difference after the seemingly insignificant journey between the gun's barrel and its grip: the barrel was free of any hint of humanity . . . it didn't smell like a man, it smelled like metal: a deeply intimidating smell, a smell you wouldn't exactly call appetizing. But when it came to the gun's grip—because of the human smell clinging to it—the smell of Hinnerk's hand—there *was* something appetizing . . . a ripe, organic smell. In addition, having made this discovery—having experienced for himself the enormous disparity between the shock of the neutral and intimidating smell of the gun barrel and the inviting (yes, inviting) smell of the gun's grip—Hinnerk came to a further realization . . . and it frightened him. He couldn't quite articulate what this realization was, but he knew there was a kind of repulsion running parallel to the thrill he'd given himself by nosing out his own smell on an object like a gun . . . yes, it was dawning on Hinnerk that, having acquired this *knowledge*, he was brushing up against a hidden horror: the possibility of one human being eating another . . . the prospect of treating another man's body as food, as something that would allow your own continued survival . . .

Because the disparity between his reactions to those two parts of the same object was clear: he felt threatened by the gun barrel and thrilled by the grip . . . and this thrill was a potpourri of familiar elements: hunger, sexual desire, and his deep, permanent dissatisfaction; a dissatisfaction that Hinnerk now found himself identifying with *appetite*, with the feeling that nothing he'd ever eaten had entirely suited him—had entirely sated him. Every day was the same . . . no matter what he'd eaten the day before, he still got hungry again—it was dull, stupid, unimaginative; Hinnerk felt disillusioned and, in a way, *deceived* by his body's organic lack of creativity. His hunger, his daily appetite, was like the hum that remains after a loud but brief noise—a noise you thought would never end, but which drops away to nothing all at once, leaving your eardrums buzzing—and then won't go away. In other words: like an obsession. Even now, after the war, he refused to believe that the human survival instinct was based wholly on the need for food. No, the need to kill—and he had experienced that need—was far nobler than the need to eat.

In wartime, one's daily bread quickly takes a backseat. Not getting killed is more important, more urgent, than eating. *I can always eat later, but I won't have a second chance to keep myself in one piece.* This urgency made hunger quite tolerable. It was hard to remember, now, what that was like.

Hinnerk had to force himself to eat. He had a certain contempt for the activity. There was no enjoyment in it. Eating was the epitome of human mediocrity. An activity almost as worthless, as tedious, as waiting. In fact, he thought, eating was a *form* of waiting—and

Hinnerk hadn't been trained to wait. He'd been trained to act. To rush at things head-on and stake his claim. He'd been a soldier on the front lines, after all—forced to stare right into the enemy guns. Danger was a privileged zone, as far as Hinnerk was concerned—a place where things *happen*; as though danger made men faster, more competent, into *doers* at last: great doers, great builders. Danger inspires us to build strong buildings—houses raised in safety seem fake, inept, ignorant of the great motivating fear that strips us bare, that reveals the truth . . . both of bricks and of human beings.

But, then, what to do with his discovery, with his delectation in the smell of his own hands? Hinnerk was confused—bent over, smelling the grip of his gun—but he felt certain, now, of a notion that had been gaining momentum in his thoughts, unnoticed, for several years . . . Hinnerk knew he would be able to eat human flesh.

And this, finally—still bent over, still smelling the grip of his gun—was what thrilled Hinnerk the most: this distancing from the world, this growing desire. He felt it inside him like a kind of talent, a supernatural power, an ability to exceed certain limits . . .

But that didn't mean his power wasn't still a bit unnerving.

2

Fifteen minutes before Hanna the whore rung his doorbell, Hinnerk
had slammed said door behind him and—with his gun, as always,
slipped between waistband and belly—headed out under the city's
streetlights.

His feet dragged, took their time choosing a route. At first, as he
left his house behind, his steps had been resolute; now they were hesi-
tant: it was almost four in the morning—where to go?

The idea of the church had probably come to him via one of those
arbitrary strings of association we're never wholly aware of—but it
had started with Hanna a few nights ago; she'd mentioned the city's
nearby church in passing: there was a boy working there as an assis-
tant to the priest, and he was one of her best customers, and one of
the least shy. A beautiful boy, in her opinion. And she went into all
the intimate details, as she often did in conversation with Hinnerk.

It was precisely those details that had piqued his curiosity. He'd
never had sex with a man; there was an obvious discomfort in him,
at certain moments, concerning the male form; but in the case of
this boy, what really caught Hinnerk's attention was the fact that—as
Hanna told him—every time the kid met up with her, he mentioned

how much he wanted to enter the priesthood. The incongruence was what Hinnerk found so interesting.

So it was probably on the basis of that conversation that Hinnerk started to head toward the area bordering the church. He wasn't really expecting to find the boy that Hanna had mentioned, of course, but he still seemed—this would have been obvious to anyone who saw him—as though he were searching for something. He felt hungry. Yes, he had an appetite. A "human appetite," in fact, he thought to himself as he walked. And the feeling of his gun against his skin calmed him down: Hinnerk was searching for something that night, and he wasn't afraid.

Chapter XII

Gomperz, Theodor

1

The walls at the Georg Rosenberg Asylum were covered in calendars. The oldest one was from ten years ago. They just never took it down. It didn't bother anyone.

Light and dark were entirely in the hands of the nurses: Matches were forbidden; there were no electrical outlets outside the common room; and after "lights-out," even the most resourceful patient couldn't have found more than one or two switches to play with.

This was a house built to do away with all mystery, as Doctor-Manager Gomperz used to say. Objects and procedures both were subject to his desire for simplicity and clarity: all items in the asylum were functional and had an easily deduced and immediate use—there was very little in plain sight that wasn't intended for daily use; if a patient managed to forget, even for a day, some object he'd previously found indispensable, this object was immediately deemed useless and unnecessary. There was, then, a sort of natural selection at work in the daily life of the asylum: whatever was deemed excessive became a therapeutic target: the asylum would try to eliminate that thing, extinguish it, banish it *outside the circle* . . . As though every life, just like an office cubicle, had its own wastepaper basket: a specific place, inconspicuously located, where all habits, actions, and, if possible, thoughts that were *not of interest* had to be thrown away—*not of interest*, that is, to the doctors. What was tossed into each individual's wastebasket wasn't chosen by the person himself, it was chosen by his or her therapy; and the hard part of this process wasn't in the *throwing away* itself—the discarding of a supposedly dangerous element of a person's life—the hard part was how to deal, then, with that little bin of toxic waste in their heads: how to bury it, forget it, keep it from contaminating the rest of your life. In the end, the number of patients who managed to learn how to forget what had been stolen from them—and thus be designated as "cured"—was very low indeed. You see, curing a patient doesn't simply mean persuading him or her to desist from certain behavior; it means helping the patient forget that there might be any way to *recover* said behavior . . . it means effacing the path that might lead back to your garbage dump.

At the Georg Rosenberg Asylum, they not only monitored the actions of their patients, they took a deep and *moral* interest in the workings of their minds: Our goal is to understand what our patients are thinking about; therapy must concentrate on the *invisible* as much as the animal.

Thus, the patients had all learned to fear Dr. Gomperz's favorite query: *What are you thinking about, my dear?*

Of course, the only one who can ever really know the answer to that sort of question is the person being asked: there's no way to force your target to be sincere; the patients could have lied and no one would have known the difference, presumably. The problem, however, wasn't that they were frightened they might blurt out the truth; the problem was that they could tell the truth all they liked and still see Dr. Gomprez assume they were lying, and then alter their therapy accordingly. There's no way to force someone to be sincere, but there's also no way to force someone else to believe you *are* being sincere. How can you prove that you're thinking what you say you're thinking?

In the final analysis, the Georg Rosenberg treatment extended from a patient's acts to his or her thoughts by way of entirely arbitrary decisions. Gomperz either believed or didn't believe that a given patient was telling the truth about thinking dangerous or unorthodox things. He was focused on the practical, the tangible; that's all that interested him.

Focused, then, on his own "minimal morality," Dr. Gomperz sometimes raised the stakes of his interrogation; asking not *what* his patient was thinking, but whether he or she knew what they *should* be thinking. He acted like a professor giving a quiz on math or grammar: there was only one correct answer possible. Even healthy people would have found it unsettling.

Theodor Busbeck, for instance—who was more than familiar with the kinds of mental entanglement a doctor can enter with a patient—found this line of questioning entirely unacceptable . . . not to mention threatening.

What should a man think about? Where should a man direct his thoughts?

2

Where should a man direct his thoughts so as not to be considered mentally ill? Such was the problem set forth by Dr. Gomperz, and which now occupied Dr. Theodor Busbeck . . .

Yes, the root of the question, of our profession—not just a matter of therapeutic practice, restricted to the treatment of the mentally ill, but a basic question of morality, concerning all mankind.

What should the moral man think about? What *shouldn't* he think about?

Of course the Church had tried to answer this question. Well before the advent of psychiatrists, it had been directing its ever-vigilant eyes not only at a man's deeds, but at his thoughts . . . and pronouncing judgment when it found these wanting. It had never been enough to act morally. One also had to have the right thoughts. The one reflected the other. And since actions proceed from thoughts, unsound actions must be taken as a symptom of incorrect thinking.

Thus, though he would never have dared say so, Dr. Gomperz's concept of madness was not medical but ethical. Simply put, a person who acts immorally is mentally ill—as is a person who acts morally, but has immoral thoughts. Madness, then, is a simple lack of ethics—either temporary, and therefore curable, or *definitive*, unending, and untreatable. The difference between criminality, so-called, and insanity, likewise so-called, was, to Gomperz, taxonomical: they were two forms of madness, and, consequently, two forms of immorality: on one hand the madness of someone driven to act in an antisocial manner, and on the other the madness of someone only minimally aware of the world in which he must act. The criminal might as easily be called a madman, and the madman, in his ignorance, is still committing a crime—even if he doesn't hurt anyone—since his actions demonstrate his own lack of understanding of the laws that govern our society. Actions taken out of ignorance are irresponsible, and irresponsibility is immoral—or so Gomperz would say. Immoral and therefore criminal.

Theodor Busbeck and Gomperz had already had a number of discussions on the subject. Though he was better known than Gomperz when it came to research, Theodor had never managed to make a name for himself as far as the *practical management of madness*—certainly not to the extent that Gomperz had at the Georg Rosenberg Asylum.

Their conversations, arguments, always masked a certain subtext, a certain accusation: Theodor thinking, *I know more than you do*; and Gomperz thinking, *I've accomplished twice as much as you*.

But despite their disagreements as to theory, the two doctors shared a cordiality that went beyond professionalism. Theodor always respected Gomperz's medical decisions regarding Mylia, his wife, no matter what he thought about his colleague's methods. Theodor had even spoken to Gomperz once or twice about the research he was carrying out parallel to his psychiatric work—trying to understand the development of horror throughout history, trying to work up a graph that might be able to foretell the dates and locations of all the next century's great tragedies. Gomperz was fascinated by Theodor's notion that one could treat all of recorded history like the case study of a single patient. Yes, his practical experience dwarfed Dr. Busbeck's—Gomperz had treated more and overall *worse* patients than Theodor—but the audacity of his graph theory was enviable. More than once Gomperz had considered abandoning his own work and offering to collaborate on Theodor's research. It was, however, easy to see that the graph project was too individual—it couldn't be shared.

Since they'd met, then, a certain mutual admiration had arisen between the two men over time . . . which, despite everything, never completely cancelled out the hostility each felt for the other—a hostility born of the unpleasant and likewise mutual suspicion that *he* (the other) *doesn't need me*. No, they didn't need each other . . . and so, they were ready to start hating one another instead.

Chapter XIII
Theodor, Gomperz, Krauss

1

He had come into Dr. Gomperz's office a few minutes before. There was an uneasiness in the air that kept each man silent. Theodor Busbeck had been summoned by one of Gomperz's secretaries. *Please be so good as to come to my office on such-and-such day at such-and-such time.* It wasn't, then, a social call. Mylia—Theodor's wife, Gomperz's patient—was the matter at hand.

Gomperz spoke at last:

"My dear Dr. Busbeck. I'll get right to the point. Believe me, I wish it weren't necessary for us to have this conversation."

Theodor was seated facing Gomperz. Gomperz was swiveling his chair from one side to another behind his desk.

"There's something wrong with Mylia," Theodor said.

"Dr. Busbeck . . . I'll try to be as frank as modesty permits. I know of course that we are both professionals, and not squeamish men, but today I need to speak to Theodor the husband, not Theodor the doctor . . . and the situation is delicate. The fact is, Dr. Busbeck, that your wife, Mylia, and another patient . . . well, they *did it*, here at the asylum. In front of the other patients. Two days ago. I'm sorry, but naturally you have a right to know. There were numerous witnesses.

Various patients, as I said, and then two nurses who later intervened. At that point they'd already been *at it* for several minutes, I'm afraid. It was the noise made by the other residents that alerted the nurses. Again, I'm very sorry.

"Of course," Gomperz continued, "you would have heard about it sooner or later regardless. You know how the patients talk. They even talk when there's nothing to talk about. And then there are the nurses. Even our nurses can't keep their mouths shut. I spent all day yesterday agonizing over how to break the news to you, but stories about your wife were already starting to go around—exaggerations, I hasten to add—so I decided to bite the bullet right away, rather than bide my time and see one of those lies reach you first. I can tell from your reaction that I was too late . . . but I assure you that I've told you everything, now: anything else you might have heard isn't true."

"Who was it?"

"You know that I can't give you that kind of information. They're all my patients, each one, and entitled to their privacy. You are only entitled to information about your wife.

"Tell me his name . . . Just his name."

"Ernst Spengler. One of our schizophrenics."

2

"He was admitted two years before your wife."

"Ernst Spengler," Theodor said.

"I hope you'll keep this information to yourself. I've broken protocol a little. I just wanted to satisfy your curiosity."

"What's wrong with him?"

"Beside being schizophrenic? I can't tell you more. And I don't see how it would help."

Gomperz slid some papers around on his desk with the tips of his fingers.

"Please don't place too much importance on what happened. You know better than I do . . ."

"You have to separate them," Theodor said brusquely, interrupting him. "They shouldn't be allowed to see each other anymore. They shouldn't be allowed to have any contact whatsoever. In any situation."

Gomperz took a deep breath. He spoke as slowly as he could:

"That's impossible, Dr. Busbeck, as you know. Certainly, according to the rules, the two of them will need to be punished in some way, but we can't prevent all contact. They're not in prison. There's a common room, there are activities groups, and so forth. It's impossible for me to do what you're asking."

"Very well," Theodor said. "I can see you want to run the Georg Rosenberg Asylum like a cheap hotel. We might as well start charging for rooms by the hour. How proud you must be of what you've accomplished here."

Another uncomfortable silence. Finally Gomperz walked over to a wooden armoire, opened a drawer, and took out two pieces of paper.

"There's one way," he said, "to arrange the conditions you desire, but it might not be . . ."

"Tell me."

"Every institution has its rules. They differ greatly, one house to another. Our own are, I think, fairer than many. In fact, I wouldn't be able to run Georg Rosenberg if I didn't think that our rules were, all things considered, best for our patients and their families both.

"Regarding Ernst, as you probably know, you have no real recourse. He's an autonomous individual, and you have no say regarding his life, despite its having intersected with your own via this regrettable incident. Regarding your wife, however, you do have some rights—that is, certain options are available to the husband of a woman who finds herself under treatment in our institution . . . For instance, we have a procedure that—between us, Doctor—we refer to as *temporary social removal*. That is, we can isolate one of our patients for a given period of time. We have three rooms designated for that purpose, and two of them are currently empty. The rooms are well equipped and kept in the best possible condition. If you like, you may inspect them. They're respectable quarters.

"We generally apply this procedure," Gomperz continued, "in situations where patients have become dangerous. That's not really the case here, but, nevertheless . . ."

"That *is* the case here, it seems to me," said Theodor Busbeck.

"That's not the case here," Gomperz repeated, raising his voice, "but I'm sure we can find a mutually agreeable solution."

A third silence. Gomperz was reading the various conditions set out in the document. Legally, these would have to be met in order for the isolation procedure to be initiated.

"My dear Busbeck," he said at last, "perhaps, yes, this incident with your wife could be considered . . . But we could only do it with your authorization. You would need to sign the application. It's not something that we do lightly. In practice, it means an isolation period of a year. While I do believe, on a therapeutic level, that the procedure might have some salubrious effects on your wife, it isn't . . ."

"I want to sign," said Theodor Busbeck.

3

Gomperz handed the document to Busbeck. He read it.

"Think it over," Gomperz said. "Take the document home. See if this is really a step you want to take."

"No thank you," said Theodor. "I'll sign it now."

"Dr. Busbeck, please."

"I'll sign it now," Theodor said.

"Dr. Busbeck, the document is valid for one year, come what may. Better to change your mind now than have second thoughts later. A year is a long time."

Theodor nodded and took a ballpoint out of his jacket.

"Please sign with this one," Gomperz said, offering him his black fountain pen.

"All set," Theodor said, handing the signed document to the director.

Theodor was on his way out.

"Dr. Busbeck . . ." Gomperz hesitated.

"Yes?"

"You won't be asking for a divorce, will you? As I said . . . this document is valid for one year. We won't be able to let Mylia back into the general population until it expires. No matter what she does, no matter how she reacts . . . and no matter if you're no longer her husband. I just wanted to make sure we agreed. It wouldn't be right to ask for a divorce under such circumstances . . ."

"No," Theodor said. "It wouldn't be right. Good afternoon, Dr. Gomperz."

4

Theodor Busbeck arrived at the office of Krauss the Lawyer, his friend, and after a bit of friendly small talk, said:

"I'd like you to initiate divorce proceedings, starting today."

Without saying another word, Krauss the Lawyer walked back to his chair, sitting at his desk and assuming the professional demeanor necessary to attend to his friend's request—and using the space of this brief journey to encourage his face to exhibit as sincere an air of utter, personal, tragic desolation as it could muster . . . without, however, overdoing it, given the offhanded way Theodor had brought the subject up. Still, it seemed essential to demonstrate how sorry he was . . . at least until he knew more.

After grabbing a piece of paper and a pen, Krauss asked—hoping he was using the right tone—"On what grounds, Theodor? Problems . . . of a psychiatric nature?"

Theodor responded right away, and without any apparent emotion:

"Adultery, actually."

Then, he corrected himself:

"Yes, psychiatric problems."

"Psychiatric problems it shall be," Krauss the Lawyer said.

5

Two months later, Theodor was called back to the Georg Rosenberg Asylum to speak with Gomperz.

"Sit down, Dr. Busbeck . . .

"My friend, here we are again. I know your divorce is moving along, and far be it from me to criticize you . . . that's not my place. I called on a related matter. I have some news for you . . . news that, shall we say . . . even taking your divorce into account . . . information that, well, *implicates* me . . .

"We're prepared to take responsibility. Nothing like this can be allowed to happen at my institution. The fact is, Dr. Busbeck, that your wife is pregnant . . ."

Chapter XIV
Gomperz, Theodor

1

"Dr. Busbeck, I repeat: we're prepared to take responsibility for this situation. I spoke with the board and it's obvious that you ought to be compensated, in some way, for this . . . unpleasantness. I trust that you won't find it necessary to complicate matters by pursuing your grievance through other channels . . . the board will know how to proceed.

"Your wife is already being gossiped about all over the hospital. The damage, on that level, has been done, and we must resign ourselves to it. Clearly, too, neither Mylia nor that man, Ernst Spengler, are in any position to raise a child . . . they're still receiving treatment, and I don't have much hope of their being discharged any time soon. Your wife, or ex-wife, is happy about the child, which I suppose is a good sign . . . and, luckily, despite what I told you earlier, the terms of the isolation procedure do in fact contain a clause permitting early termination of said procedure in case of pregnancy; thus, I'm happy to report that Mylia is back in her old room, and has been allowed to mingle with the general population. I would have informed you earlier, but, as I said, given her pregnancy, your authorization wasn't necessary, as I'm sure you'll understand.

"Quite apart from whatever compensation you might be owed, we'd like you to consider the fate of the child. In light of the fact that Mylia is, or was, your wife . . . you could, if you like, assume paternity. But I don't think anyone would expect this of you, in light of recent events. To make matters worse, I am obliged to inform you that the child will almost certainly be born with certain physical defects.

"Whatever your decision, the Georg Rosenberg Asylum will stand behind you—we'll consider it correct, justified, and definitive. Further, as your colleague, allow me to point out, at this difficult moment, that whatever your choice, it will, by nature, be ethically irreproachable."

2

Gomperz stopped talking and took a deep breath. Here he was, sitting in his chair, behind his desk, having a difficult conversation with Dr. Busbeck—one of the country's most promising theorists in the field of mental health—for the second time in just a few months. Busbeck still hadn't said a word; he was leaning forward slightly as though being scolded: the facts themselves were a kind of recrimination. Gomperz watched Theodor, fascinated with the spectacle of a brilliant mind attempting to defy reality, to negate the events of the recent past, which had, unexpectedly, slipped completely out of its control. Life had brutally sabotaged Theodor's careful plans—that much was obvious—and had become something alien to him now, stripped of theory and operating entirely without his consent . . .

The influence of one's surroundings, Gomperz thought with a certain malicious delight—even suppressing a smile. No matter how brilliant you are, you're still a product of your environment . . .

Which isn't to say that Gomperz didn't feel pity for his colleague. He did—though it was an abstract and rather futile sensation, since Gomperz was still in a position of strength; despite having acknowledged his own responsibility, as doctor-director of the asylum, for the failure in vigilance that had caused their problem, he didn't feel any particular emotional involvement in it. Yes, it couldn't be denied, Gomperz had failed on an important professional level, but this didn't really affect his life in any meaningful way . . . as opposed, that is, to Theodor's. For Gomperz, this was a failure that could be erased. A failure that could be erased with money.

The paradox here was that Theodor, who wasn't responsible for the mess he'd found himself in—or not especially—was himself facing all its most serious consequences; his own failure—in managing to keep this disruption at a distance, in finding himself forced again to participate in the world—could not be bought off. This was a decisive moment; truly an invitation for Theodor to become, again, a member of the species he was so determined to save. It felt like a punishment. Why him? Why now? Someone who'd gradually removed himself from the circumstances of life, who for many years now had been immersed in important research into individual and universal madness; someone who, from time to time, published a scientific article that, within days, set off countless responses and attacks, influencing every branch of his field . . . someone of that intellectual caliber understands that the table of reality isn't set for him and him alone . . . Other people eat too, Theodor told himself, and they're welcome to it. Why am I being forced to eat another man's share?

Gomperz had no interest in such speculation. He waited for Theodor to speak. The Director had carried out his mission; now he had to wait in silence. The longer he was made to wait, the more he found himself savoring the experience: what a privilege it was to see the practical world—which he felt he represented—infiltrate and contaminate the pride of a man who had believed he could live, from beginning to end, without ever really needing anyone else . . . and without ever being needed. My dear Theodor, thought Gomperz, it's all over now . . . *they've thrown themselves in your path.* You can't just continue on as usual—you have to make a decision, and you have to make it alone . . . no graphs or theories allowed.

Gomperz did his best to suppress his enjoyment; he held his breath, kept his face as blank as possible; it was, in all honesty, a tremendous effort: there was a perverse streak in the Director—which he recognized, and of which he wasn't especially proud—and it was straining to come out. Gomperz remembered some of the graphs that Busbeck had shown him in the past, during their conversations about his thesis—graphs marking out the distribution of all those little "surprises" in world history—and he wished now he could slap them down on the table, look the illustrious researcher in the eye, and say: Remember these? Let's see you graph your way out of *this* little surprise . . .

How delightful it was to be present at the very moment Busbeck's theory was disproved. If Theodor couldn't foresee what was about to happen in his own life—or happen to the person he was meant to be closest to, emotionally—how could he hope to tell us anything about the rest of the world, about all his precious centuries?

What—still can't decide, my dear Theodor? Gomperz snickered to himself. The smile he'd tried to suppress had now made its way onto his lips, though he wasn't aware of it—a malicious smile, an evil smile. *Still can't decide, little Einstein? Then what good, exactly, is that brilliant mind of yours? Oh, Theodor Busbeck, if you could only see the look on your face! Frankly, my friend, it's the look of an imbecile . . . Impossible! you'd say, but there it is, right in front of me—so pale, frozen in terror, like an ignoramus called to the blackboard. Oh, my dear Theodor Busbeck, if a rat were to crawl into my office and climb up onto your*

shoulders, scurry all around that brilliant head of yours, casually brushing its long tail against your nose, you wouldn't even notice, you wouldn't
even protect yourself—too busy thinking! But rats don't sit and wait po-
litely for you to finish thinking—they act, my dear Theodor, they're there,
under our feet, their little legs always moving, their little snouts rifling
through all the shit we leave around us, climbing in and out of every hole
we've left open for them, just as much at home in the trenches as in a
library—violence or culture, it's all the same to them. Yes, my dear Theodor Busbeck, if only you could see your face right now—and speaking
of rats, I can't help but notice that there's a ratlike quality to your own
august self . . . you have the face of a rat, dear colleague! How obvious,
now that I've made the connection . . . Busbeck the ratlike researcher
nibbling his way through all of world history! You want to show your
fellow rats the error of their ways . . . want to prove that a library isn't a
trench and vice versa . . . but you've failed, you know . . . it can't be done!
You're no better a rat than you are a human being, my dear Busbeck.
Perhaps you'd better take a little vacation. You need to recharge your
rat-batteries. What a mess you've made of your life. Just look at yourself.
Your veins are all popping out, I can see them now, they're bulging under
your skin . . . My dear Theodor, please calm yourself . . . this is the su-
preme moment! You can't just drop dead just when life is finally singling
you out! Rise to the occasion! Make a decision!

"Would you like a glass of water, Dr. Busbeck?"

Busbeck shook his head.

*Come now, Dr. Rat . . . no more mistakes. You can't afford them.
Have a drink. Refuel. You need it.*

"I'm going to get you a glass of water," Gomperz said tactfully.
"You're going pale."

But Theodor Busbeck stood up.

"Thank you, Dr. Gomperz. I appreciate your kindness, but I've made my decision. I'll keep the child. Please, make sure that the child is identified as mine on all the necessary paperwork. I hope you'll take very good care of my ex-wife until the child is born. After that, I'll send someone to come get it. As far as compensation, naturally I won't turn down the board's offer . . . I think that three million would be the right amount—enough to keep my next article from ruining the excellent reputation of the Georg Rosenberg Asylum. Thank you very much for your time, Dr. Gomperz. When next we meet, I hope it will be under less complicated circumstances."

Theodor Busbeck left the office after a quick and vigorous hand-shake, and Gomperz let himself fall into his chair. Three million! It was his turn, now, to go pale.

Chapter XV
Europa 02

1

Theodor left his seven-year-old son, Kaas Busbeck, at school as usual and, seated at one of the tables at the library, was preparing to get back to his research concerning this or that period of history when his attention was diverted by a work of fiction that the librarian had left on his table with the note: *This might interest you, Doctor.* The book was called *Europa 02.*

Busbeck flipped through it: it looked like a catalog. He chose a page at random, read it, and continued in that fashion: leafing through, skipping ahead, going back.

(I)

Excluded

He who makes a mistake is excluded. Is enclosed inside a box. He who is outside can hardly see the box. But the person who is enclosed, excluded, is able to see the outside. He sees everything, he sees all of us.

In each compartment there are dozens of boxes. Thousands of boxes overall. Most are empty. Others contain the excluded. Nobody knows which boxes are which.

The boxes are so numerous that no one pays any attention to them. There could be a person in there, perhaps even someone you love, but you don't bother to look. You don't even see them anymore. You pass them hundreds of times a day.

(II)

Search

When the whistle blows, you have ten minutes to return to your compartment. To the few square meters that belong to you.

After that, you can't leave, and no one else can come in.

Once they've completed the search, they let you out again. For some people, the Search only takes ten minutes. For others, ten days.

You can be trapped in your space for days. Waiting. After it seems a long time has passed, and you hear other people moving freely in the hallways, you begin to become anxious. You think you've been forgotten.

What they search is your body, the visible parts of you. They take your measurements. They take samples of everything your body produces. They also search your things; they keep a count of all the objects you have in your space. They take photographs of everything from different angles. They double-check their figures. They verify whether there's anything in your compartment that doesn't belong to you. Or anything that's missing.

(III)

Law

You can follow all their rules to the letter, but, sooner or later, they'll show up with a short legal document, and then you'll understand: you've been sentenced to death.

What they do is arbitrary, but never illegal. The first thing they do is show you the law that they are following, the document that has determined their action.

No one fights it. People accept the law. If they didn't, things would only be worse.

(IV)

Medical exams are carried out in public places.

You take a seat. Suddenly, they tap you on the shoulder and say: your turn. You get up immediately, lean against the wall, and fall apart.

At each Medical Exam they mark a cross on the back of your hand. There are people who've already had dozens. And everyone knows that you're only chosen for an examination if you're diseased.

Since the backs of their hands are marked, some try to keep their palms facing up at all times. But they give themselves away with this gesture. It makes them seem even more disgusting than they already might. The others distance themselves.

Medical Examination

(V)

Instruments

They never touch you. They do their work through the tips of their instruments. They contaminate you with the tips of their instruments. You can't really see anything at all, and yet the tips of their instruments seem to be covered in a coarse powder.

Until you feel the instruments, you aren't afraid. Afterward, you are.

(VI)

Medical Examination

Sometimes they just like to scare you. They open a gash in your skin and then close it up again. They arrange their instruments on a tray. They say: No sickness. Then they smile. They walk away, and you start to get dressed.

Other times, it's different. They make tiny incisions. They touch you with their instruments. They take little things out of your body. It doesn't matter what. It doesn't hurt.

(VII)

Displacement You suddenly lose touch with a person that you used to greet every day. You no longer know where he is. He could have been Excluded into a box or he could have been killed. Or, Displaced to a compartment far away.

(VIII)

Diseases

They hunt for strange diseases. They hunt for sick people who are themselves strange. Whoever is found to have a strange disease is no longer a sick person, however. Now he is a criminal.

Having a regular disease means one that has been obedient and dutiful in his work. A strange disease is a sign of failure: a lack of personal hygiene. A lack of honesty.

(IX)

Displacement

The first time they make us do it, or when they make us do it to someone we know, they grab our hands forcefully and guide them. We have to do it. No one refuses. They grab our hands forcefully and direct them so that we don't shake. So that we don't fail. So that we torture with precision.

They can call you in any place and at any moment. You hear: Torture.

They can decide that you'll be the victim, or decide that you'll be the torturer. You don't need to have done anything wrong. They choose you at random to make you suffer.

When they say Torture, you never know if they're calling you do the torturing or be tortured.

You have to follow them, after they call you. You can torture, or be tortured. There's no third alternative. In the end, you hope you'll be the torturer.

The torture is carried out in the compartment of the person who's been chosen as the torturer. Because of this, when you see that you're being herded towards your own space, you can't help but feel exultant: you clench your fists and growl in satisfaction.

You don't know who your victim will be until you enter your compartment. It could be a stranger, but it could also be a friend, or someone you love. Then you'll feel disgust, not so much at the torture itself, which you can't help, but at the happiness you felt moments before, when you realized that you wouldn't be the victim; an instinctive happiness that acted independently of your conscience, and which, because of that, will go on disgusting you for a very long time.

Chapter XVI
Theodor

1

Theodor Busbeck closed *Europa 02*, irritated. He pushed the thing away, to the far side of his table, and went back to the books he'd been planning to spend his day on.

A concentration-camp survivor had said: "Normal men don't know that everything is possible." Theodor underlined the sentence.

On another page, he read:

"A Jew released from Buchenwald once discovered among the SS men who gave him the certificates of release a former schoolmate, whom he did not address but yet stared at. Spontaneously the man stared at remarked: You must understand, I have five years of unemployment behind me. They can do anything they want with me."

Theodor transcribed that passage in his notebook. The link between unemployment and horror. He would have to go through the records of unemployment rates over various periods of history. This raised a question, however: five centuries ago, what would have been considered unemployment? It's easy to define what was or was not a massacre, but unemployment, as a concept, is somewhat more ambiguous. Deaths can be hidden, of course—millions of mass graves were still waiting to be discovered—but once brought to light, death is a fact that doesn't really leave much room for interpretation: a corpse is a corpse. Unemployment, on the other hand . . . how many jobless months or years need to pass before one qualifies? What about a man who works one hour a week? It would be virtually impossible to settle on a universally acknowledged standard. Nevertheless, it was imperative for his project that Theodor root out the connection between unemployment and horror—their effect, that is, on a cross-section of easily influenced units of society: to what degree would the unemployed sympathize with the victims of a given horror?—and then, how likely was it that they would, in the end, join the ranks of the oppressors? Theodor had an intuition—despite not having the data to back it up as yet—that there were probably unemployed people on both sides of the question: perpetrators and victims. It's a heartless way to think about it, but perpetrating horror is an activity . . . as is being the victim of horror. Two activities, two actions. An axiom—perhaps a little facile?—began to sketch itself out in Theodor's mind: horror is work that puts an end to work; useful activity, whatever it may be, is derailed by the survival instinct when horror comes calling . . . the survival instinct, that is, or else that other instinct, just as human: the instinct to oppress, to brutalize. Nobody bakes bread while he's being tortured, and you would only bake bread *while torturing* if you were indulging in some kind of sick joke . . . That much was clear; in fact, painfully obvious . . . But the essential thing was to figure out whether a given set of victims and oppressors were—if not employed in the usual sense—then *active* before a particular horror commenced; whether, Theodor thought, *they had been focused on something else.* Could a man who was truly *involved* in some common, constructive, let's say "harmless" activity turn into a murderer overnight? That was the question . . . and Theodor Busbeck formulated it as follows: *Could*

someone excited by his stamp collection or the possibility of having a
newly discovered comet named after himself turn into an engine of hor-
ror between one morning and the next?

Theodor went back to his Arendt: ". . . six million Jews, six million human beings, were helplessly, and in most cases unsuspect-
ingly, dragged to their deaths. The method employed was that of ac-
cumulated terror . . . Last came the death factories—and they all died
together, the young and the old, the weak and the strong, the sick
and the healthy; not as people, not as men and women, children and
adults, boys and girls . . . but brought down to the lowest common
denominator of organic life itself . . . like cattle . . ."

Theodor took a deep breath. He was steeling himself to continue
his reading when he heard someone whisper his name. A man came
over to him, bending over to speak:

"Dr. Theodor Busbeck?"

"Yes?"

"It's your father. He's dying."

Chapter XVII
Kaas, Hinnerk

1

Kaas Busbeck was twelve years old, and had never been out on the street alone at this time of night. He felt fear trickle down his body . . . parents say "good night! sweet dreams!" after finishing a bedtime story . . . but this was not a sweet dream, and the night, Kaas had discovered, was not good at all . . . night was horrible . . . perhaps even malevolent.

His shoulders were hunched, protesting the cold: he'd left in a hurry, his jacket wasn't enough.

He was out on the street, he was only a child, but he had a mission: his father, Theodor Busbeck, a respected doctor, had gone out in the middle of the night, leaving him all alone. His mission was to keep his fear under control and find his father.

Kaas was already imagining their reunion. He would reproach Theodor publicly; he would shout, he would demand respect. It wasn't appropriate, what Theodor had done, leaving his son alone. His son was only twelve years old and had very, very skinny legs. Kaas was pretty sure it was even illegal, what Theodor had done.

Kaas was walking at an unusually determined pace. He'd managed to forget about his legs in his outrage. Careless, with a mixture of fear and expectation, his gait only accentuated his handicaps; if anyone had been awake to see him, they would've laughed.

The perfect, unnatural orderliness of the streets was some comfort. Kaas's steps, nominally following a straight line, were expressions of animal confusion, constrained by the structure of a grid: in all the city's straight lines, nearly trafficless now, there was a feeling of safety . . . as if nothing horrible could happen in such an artificial environment.

There was a recklessness in Kaas. It came from being so overprotected, as he was by the entire Busbeck family, though mainly by his father. Twelve years are more than enough for most animals to learn how to navigate in the world, but in Kaas's case they'd been of little use; there, at night—an entirely foreign state of affairs for the boy, where darkness multiplied the likelihood of an unexpected encounter by a factor of thousands—Kaas didn't even understand that it was safer to walk in the middle of the street rather than the sidewalk, since, the more space you keep around you, the more warning you have if anything dangerous comes your way. Kaas was naïve, in other words: at four in the morning, alone, in the middle of the city, he was still more worried about being hit by a car than about the damage another human being might do . . .

Kaas walked on. There aren't many questions to ask at night. The movements of his body, however comic, were automatic, self-correcting. He tried, distractedly, to think up what he would say to his father to reproach him for his actions. The father who had forgotten him.

As he pushed onward, his right leg began to drag; Kaas wasn't used to this kind of sustained exertion. It had been years since the boy had bothered taking an interest in his body . . . despite his father's encouragement, despite the physical therapy he still received, despite the gymnastics classes. He knew he'd never be athletic: that his legs—and his speech too, another defect—were more or less hopeless. He tried to live as though he had no body. He wasn't even interested in the little tricks and feats of endurance children perform in order to impress one another . . . things his handicaps wouldn't have interfered with, like bending one finger all the way back. He'd learned very early that he needed to protect his body from other people's eyes—to hide it. As a result, he'd even managed to hide it from himself.

Already exhausted, then, forced to slow down, he was still a good distance from the center of town when he ran into Hinnerk Obst.

2

Hinnerk Obst: motivated distantly by Hanna's story about that boy-client of hers who saw no contradiction between his religious and sexual aspirations. Hinnerk Obst: still conscious of his terrifying, so-called "human appetite"—particularly sharp that night, almost painful—stabbing away at the chest. Yes, Hinnerk had already been watching Kaas for a few minutes now, taking in his halting movements. At first glance, he thought the boy must have fallen—hence the dragging motion—but he quickly realized that the kid was handicapped. Hinnerk noticed Kaas's thin, his very thin legs.

"Evening, kid," Hinnerk Obst said.

Kaas stopped. This was the first man he'd seen since setting off after his father. Perhaps he would help him. He tried to say a word, but it came out as *Blufscruk*.

Kaas waved this word away and shook his head apologetically. Then he concentrated, saying, "Busbeaaak" and pointing at his chest, as though trying to make himself understood in a foreign language.

"My father," he managed. "Busbeaaaaaak."

Kaas extended the name, distorting it, its two syllables interminable. His speech impediment wasn't quite a stutter—the morphology of his mangled language was dissimilar in every respect to that other, relatively common complaint—but sometimes, in certain words, the effects were rather similar.

"You're looking for your father, is that it?" Hinnerk asked.

Kaas answered with a drawn out *Yyes*.

"It's not a good idea to walk around here alone at night," Hinnerk said, putting his hand on the kid's neck affectionately. "Let's go," he added, and pulled him along. "I'm sure your father is around here somewhere."

Chapter XVIII
Theodor, Kaas

1

Theodor Busbeck, at the library, jumped up.

"It's your father. He's dying."

He stacked the books and documents he had been looking at and put his things back into his briefcase.

"Let's go," he said.

Theodor's father, Thomas Busbeck, had been confined to a hospital bed for several months; as such, the news hadn't come as a complete surprise . . . it was more a nuisance, really, since it had interrupted Theodor's research. He tried, however, to channel his irritation into some other, more appropriate emotion before it was noticed.

"Is he still talking?" Theodor asked the messenger, who had now identified himself as a hospital orderly.

"Yes," the messenger responded. "He asked us to call his son, the doctor."

Theodor's mother had died the previous year. Now it seemed his father's time had come as well. The last living vessel of Theodor Busbeck's individual, biological history was about to disappear—but that was cause for relief. The more his private history was effaced, the more Theodor would be able to concentrate on public history, on the history of all mankind, on the history of the human mind and its pathologies. To Theodor, the death of a father was no more devastating than a bit of necessary housekeeping, putting his affairs in order: a maid clearing an old piece of furniture out of the way, one that he'd been bumping into for decades.

"He won't last more than a few hours," the messenger told Theodor.

"Yes," Theodor said. "A tragedy."

2

And yet, while he was walking to the hospital, Theodor felt a vague disturbance at the center of the feeling of orderliness that the news about his father had brought him. Gradually, the disturbance came into focus: Theodor had forgotten about his son, Kaas.

Theodor stopped.

"My son Kaas is at school. He's seven years old. I have to go get him. We'll head straight to the hospital from there."

"Your father might not last that long."

"I'm going to get my son before I do anything else," Theodor said quickly. "We'll head straight to the hospital from there."

Chapter XIX
Theodor, Kaas, Thomas

1

Theodor and his son Kaas shuffled into the room of Thomas Busbeck, a man who—thirty years before—had been one of the most famous people in the country. Now he was simply dead.

Thirty years before, when Thomas Busbeck wanted to talk to someone, he never had to wait. The whole city had been at his disposal—as though everyone always set an extra place at their tables, just in case Thomas wanted to honor them with his presence.

Thomas Busbeck had been one of the most influential politicians in the country. The cornerstone of his career had been simple stubbornness: a tactic that came to seem more and more praiseworthy each year he managed to stay in office; the ideals and alliances of his rivals—who had once seemed indestructible—proving as flimsy as old rags beside him. He was always on his own: he never went to anyone else for help, never asked another man to back him up—since he could never accept that any other man might be his equal. When he *did* face defeat, Thomas simply redoubled his efforts, coming back even stronger than before—finding that losing a battle here and there actually made him *more* popular, over time, giving his words a new, hard-won dependability. And as the years went by, when he lost at all, he lost by a smaller margin each election, until the day he ran for mayor and finally won himself the entire city. Five years later, the country's leading magazine declared him "Man of the Year."

Men and women had clearly defined roles in the Busbeck family: men worked to *get* things and women worked to *keep* them; like different regiments in an occupying army: one to go out and conquer, the other to take on the extremely difficult and delicate job of keeping the ground thus won . . . in other words: the women held the responsibility for maintaining the Busbeck name—*fame without notoriety*, as they put it. No woman in the family would be ashamed to say: I keep my husband's fame unsullied. And why be ashamed? Success is success.

2

Old Thomas Busbeck's wife, Theodor's mother, had died the year before. Like her husband, she spent her final months in bed—though
her own bed, in the family house. Once, back in those days when
his grandmother was *permanently resting*, Kaas had seen something,
accidentally—something that he would never fully understand.

It happened like this: Kaas, who was barely six years old, had made
his ungainly way to the door of the servant's quarters—unseen, as
he'd done many times before. He opened the door a crack and saw
his grandfather, Thomas Busbeck, sitting on the maid's bed. Her head
was between his grandfather's legs, moving in a way that Kaas understood, somehow, to be perfectly monstrous.

"Get out of here, you idiot!" Old Busbeck yelled.

So Kaas turned around and fled.

Hours later, after a brief conversation with the boy's grandfather, Theodor called him.

Kaas was frightened by the look on his father's face and tried to
say something—unintelligible. Theodor asked his son to come closer,
and when Kaas obeyed, he hit him, hard.

Then he said: "You need to learn to speak properly."

3

"You see?" Theodor asked, lifting his son up to get a better look. "You see? It's your grandfather. He's dead."

That day, for the first time, Kaas saw his grandfather Thomas from above. *Like I was in a helicopter*, he said later. His grandfather was silent and still, eyes closed, arms across his torso: right hand placed over left hand.

Kaas, still up in the air, in his father's arms, bewildered at the arrangement of the corpse, pointed at his grandfather and asked (garbled as ever):

"Is he afraid of something?"

Chapter XX
Thomas, Theodor, Kaas

1

When Theodor had told his father he was going to marry Mylia—one of his patients—Thomas's reaction, after a long silence, was:

"That woman is going to ruin your reputation."

Thomas Busbeck took a certain pleasure, later, in seeing this prediction borne out.

First came the news that his daughter-in-law was going to be committed to the Georg Rosenberg Asylum. After all the friction in the couples' life, this news was received without surprise.

"It's the only solution," old Thomas had said.

Months later, the news of the divorce and of Mylia's pregnancy broke at almost the same time.

Theodor let his father believe that the child was legitimate. The mother had no rights. As soon as the child was born, he was handed over to the Busbeck family.

It wasn't long, however, before old Busbeck saw that something wasn't right with the boy—the boy he'd imagined would carry on the family name. Theodor was Thomas's only son, but a shrink was . . . not ideal. Kaas was the last hope for the family, if the magnificence of the Busbecks was to be recognized by future generations.

"The family line can't end with someone who studies crazy people," Thomas would say to Theodor, "brilliant or not. At the very least it should end with someone who studies crazy kings and emperors . . ."

That the subject of Theodor's research changed over time from practical therapeutics to *the pathology of evil throughout history* was very likely the result of his father's influence. When Theodor described his research to Thomas for the first time, spelling out some of his hypotheses about the evolution of violence, the old man had rejoiced:

"Now *that's* a topic for a Busbeck!"

But Theodor could only do so much. As Kaas grew older, Thomas grew more and more disappointed in him, despite the affection he claimed to have for the boy. Finally, when Kaas was four years old, Thomas brought matters to a head: he and Theodor were in the living room; they'd spent nearly two hours embroiled in a game of chess—something that always brought out a strong competitive instinct in both men. With the stalemate no closer to being resolved, Thomas suddenly abandoned the game; he stood, went to the liquor cabinet, and poured himself a glass.

"Theodor," the elder Busbeck said, "you're my only son. Look at our faces: yours and mine. There are dozens of ways to know who is and isn't a member of one's family . . . Simple ways, obvious ways. Our faces, for example, leave no room whatsoever for doubt. You look exactly as I did thirty years ago. And, believe me, I'm proud of what I looked like thirty years ago."

Theodor was standing now too, almost out of respect. His father had an air of almost imperial authority, all of a sudden: he'd stuck out his chest and straightened his back—an obvious power-display—and was holding his glass as though the base object wasn't worthy of being touched by his hands. It was clear that Thomas Busbeck was in high dudgeon.

"Theodor," the old man said finally, "the boy isn't yours. It's obvious. I tried to warn you a long time ago, years ago . . . I told you that that woman would ruin you. Now she's done exactly that. Everyone in the city knows the story. When you walk down the street with Kaas, people make fun of him—and they make fun of you."

A long pause.

"I like the boy," said Thomas, "but he's not my grandson. It's time for you to repair your error. There are plenty of places you could put him. Places where children like him receive better treatment than you could ever provide the poor thing."

Thomas drank what was left in his glass.

"You're just starting out, all in all. You're well known. Your thesis about health and the search for God—or whatever it is—has gotten a lot of attention. Your colleagues criticize you, yes, but it's clear that they're absolutely terrified. They can already tell that you're not just another rival: you're going to be *better* than them. So why give them ammunition? Why help them do you harm? Do you really think they'll hesitate to exploit this weakness? Look: I don't claim to have any special insights into the minds of men, Doctor, but you know I've met more than my share, and, to put it in your language, sample size is hardly irrelevant . . . I've watched hundreds of people betray me to my face, and more than hundreds do it behind my back. The same thing is going to happen to you . . .

"Remember, Theodor, that you're a Busbeck. You must distinguish yourself among your fellow men—and no one can help you do it. Your mother would have done anything for you, of course, no matter what, but she's in her bed now, and won't ever get up. I don't have many years left myself—and you ought to know that I won't jeopardize what I've built to save a man from his own blindness and folly . . . not even my own son.

"You need to make very certain that your work can continue without interference. That woman that you made the mistake of marrying . . . she ruined your life a little, but what's left is salvageable. You left her—very good. You did what you could to wipe away that error. But there's still a stain on you . . . the child. It's early yet: he's young. He hasn't contaminated things completely. Don't think that your colleagues will admire you for bringing up a cripple who isn't even yours. What they'll say is that a crazy woman cheated on you with another crazy person. That's all. The Busbecks were born to mock, Theodor . . . not to be the objects of mockery."

2

Kaas, like any living creature, could only suffer so much without striking back. Once, Theodor, who was pretending to be asleep in a small adjoining room, saw his son, who was four years old then, sitting parallel to his grandmother—who had already gone almost completely blind—on her bed. The family dog was roaming around between the two of them, and Kaas's grandmother, ancient, holding her useless walking stick in hand, was taunting the animal, which she felt brushing up against her legs. She reached out from time to time, trying to poke the creature with her stick, but kept missing, and so began to call the dog's name sweetly so as to coax it back into range. Kaas, who was four, laughed at the old lady who didn't know where the dog was, and then, for no apparent reason, snuck off the bed, climbed in behind his grandmother, made a fist, and punched her square in the back. Theodor saw everything, stifling his impulse to intervene; he lay still with his eyes half-closed, watching. His mother gave a little yell at Kaas's punch, and the boy laughed, slipping off the bed, yelling something as he crossed the room. The old woman couldn't make head or tail of it, but Theodor understood what his son was trying to say: in Kaas's usual tortured way, and with what might even have been ridicule in his voice, the boy was shouting: *It was the dog, it was the dog!*

Now Theodor's mother was trying with all her might to brain *someone, anyone* with her walking stick, waving it up and down and in every direction she could manage. Perhaps she knew, at heart, that her grandson and dog weren't near enough to hit, but all the same, given her state of health, she was out for blood, swinging her stick with enviable strength, hard enough to do real damage—knocking over nearby chairs and beating dust out of the carpet.

Nevertheless, Theodor saw four-year-old Kaas sneak around the danger zone—dragging himself forward on those unnaturally tiny legs of his—climb back into the bed behind his grandmother, and then—as she was straining forward, trying to understand what was happening to her—deliver as hard a punch as his right arm could manage, again in the old Busbeck woman's back . . . his little face alight all the while with a look of hideous satisfaction.

3

Theodor was outlining a cautious hypothesis regarding the probability of unemployment affecting the human instinct toward violence, as well as the instinct toward the opposite of violence—the kindness or compassion that erupts *mysteriously* in certain people at certain times, causing them to abandon their individual projects to focus on the common good. That is, what was occupying Theodor's mind as he held his son over his father's deathbed—his son Kaas who was seven years old and had been pulled out of school that day to watch his grandfather die—was the notion that good and evil might have their origins in inactivity and boredom, and, as such, that concrete, specialized, individually directed activity generated what might be termed a morally neutral attitude toward the world. If so, simple activity—*work*, to be precise—could be employed as a means of avoiding the horrors of history, its great massacres; though, at the same time, one would have to accept that this constant *busyness* would also remove the conditions necessary for the emergence of any grand, heroic, or noble gestures . . . so that our great holy men would disappear along with our great butchers. Still, over the last ten centuries, acts of good, so-called, were clearly not as significant as acts of pure evil: the latter were the engine of history, driving us forward, while the former were isolated incidents. There are no moral or immoral engines, Theodor thought: there are only engines that work and move things forward and engines that don't. Historically, holiness doesn't accomplish anything—and that was, for Theodor, an important realization. Progress was solely dependent, it seemed, on the *velocity of evil*. He was so satisfied with this summation that, when an orderly came up to him to say that Thomas Busbeck had only just died a few minutes before his son's arrival, Theodor responded firmly and unequivocally:

"Excellent! Excellent!"

Chapter XXI
Hinnerk, Kaas, Ernst, Mylia

1

The twelve-year-old boy who could neither speak nor walk properly and who was looking for his father in the middle of the night was getting more and more frightened. Now that the man with the enormous bags under his eyes had grabbed the back of his neck, Kaas was so scared he couldn't even react.

Hinnerk pulled him toward a side street, almost completely dark.

"Your father . . . Busbaak, was that it?"

Kaas was shaking. This strange man was no good, and the two of them had now left the relatively well-traveled—and well-lit—street where they'd met. And yet, Kaas still found himself thinking of his father, Theodor Busbeck. He'd had no right to leave his son alone; Theodor knew very well that Kaas might need him in the middle of the night. Theodor had betrayed his son. Kaas wouldn't let him get away with it. It just wasn't smart, the boy thought, for a grown man to go off in the middle of the night like that.

Hinnerk continued to pull the kid, as delicately as possible, behind a building. No light at all now. Kaas was startled into abandoning his silent condemnation of his father and made a feeble attempt to loosen the man's grip on his neck. In response, Hinnerk threw him to the ground.

Kaas did his best to scream.

2

Meanwhile, Ernst was by the phone booth, crouched over Mylia. She was just coming to.

Ernst touched her cheek gently with his index finger, by her right eye. Nocturnal scares are particularly intense . . . a little light, however, reveals things as they are.

Mylia saw that the voice she'd heard on the phone had now incarnated itself in a body . . . a body that was touching her at that very moment. How was that possible?

Everything in her life, Mylia decided, had been touched by divine intervention. Ernst had found her because he was travelling *an indirect route* back into her life, guided by God. "The soul of a just man will declare truths more clearly than seven sentinels . . ."

Yes, the facts were clear—and God was clearly visible in them. When you touched me, Mylia said, or thought, to Ernst, I recognized your hand before I even opened my eyes.

She looked at him, serene and meticulous: Ernst trembling as always, his head shaking from side to side, *like a crazy person*, Mylia thought. She was content, she found, all of a sudden—it's hard to hate yourself, hard to see yourself as worthless, when a loved one rushes to your side in your moment of distress. A loved one from your past, no less. Besides, Mylia thought, hate is dangerous . . . more dangerous than war. When questions end, hate begins. She'd heard Theodor say that, once.

So, "Where have you been?" she asked Ernst.

Perhaps a poor choice. As questions go, it was both cautious and intrusive, almost violent. *Where have you been*? Did she mean: What streets have you been walking down, what houses have you been living in? No. An ontological question, not a geographical one. *We're not talking about a leisurely stroll.*

But it was easy to read, in Ernst's nervous face, how little had changed for him since they'd last met. He hadn't been anywhere.

Mylia thought, "If I forget thee, O Jerusalem, let my right hand wither . . ."

They embraced.

Chapter XXII
Gomperz, Mylia, Lanz, Godicke,
Wisliz, Gada, Thinka, Witold

1

When Dr. Gomperz called Mylia into his office, he was holding his black notebook, where he recorded—incessantly, automatically, almost as a nervous habit—essential data about the progress of his "guests."

Mylia had given birth two weeks ago. There were celebrations in the kitchen to mark the event: the cooking staff drinking cooking wine out of the only glasses available—too small to contain the libations their enormous excitement called for—bumping into the tables and generally making fools of themselves. They had the excuse of a baby, a real "homegrown baby," the very first the asylum had ever known—though, naturally, they had to keep their festivities out of sight, unofficial; they were still Georg Rosenberg employees, after all, and so responsible for "decency," as the Director put it. But: surely they had the right to enjoy themselves once and a while, as long as it didn't get out of hand? The monotony of Georg Rosenberg routine had finally been disrupted . . . and for the low-ranking employees, this was truly something to celebrate.

Otherwise, the only creative outlet open to the kitchen staff was "presentation" . . . the way their institutional cooking could be arranged on the plates the waitstaff would then place, gently, in front of each patient at mealtimes. Sometimes they were even complimented for their trouble: *Good cook, good food*. Food was something everyone at the asylum was expected to treat with respect—as though it were an old man with gray hair who needed a little help getting around.

Nothing—including food—was exempt from the order and discipline of the Georg Rosenberg Asylum: an enforced tranquility that extended into every room, ending not at the walls of the main building but extending as far as what a patient might be able to see through its reinforced windows; as though the scenery itself had been enlisted to transmit the Director's message of restraint and equanimity in all things: don't look too much, please, *look only in moderation*; as though a patient could somehow exhaust himself trying to see what was outside; as though even sight took its toll on the body, and thus ought to be discouraged. Yes, everything at the Georg Rosenberg Asylum operated under the rule of constraint, containment: the world beyond the asylum grounds was chaotic, childish in its exhibitionism, and thus totally unsuited to the gravity, the maturity, and the control the Director required of his patients—and had instituted upon the natural world within his domain.

One of the patients kept repeating, "The outside is wet!"

Whenever it rained, some of the water would collect in the uneven tiles on the roof of the asylum, splashing to the ground past the common-room window with a sudden, comic intensity minutes or hours after the rain itself had stopped—a little "liquid entertainment" for anyone who might have missed the excitement of the actual storm. Those uneven tiles, all concentrated on one side of the building, represented—before the child—one of the only two volatile elements in the asylum's steady, daily rhythm: a concession to the anarchy of nature, which responded in kind with storm after storm, providing whatever reservoir or circuit was hidden up in the roof the means to stage a revolt against the mortal stagnation that reigned below.

Those miniature waterfalls represented an *infusion of health*, real health, which is capricious and violent, not serene and monotonous: a health that was the opposite of boredom, of regularity, of the pills that the doctors seemed to have confused with nutrition, since they were served to their patients far more often than food—even supplanting food entirely in some cases, overwhelming a patient's desire for rice or meat—which, admittedly, wasn't especially well cooked at the asylum, usually coming out overcooked and tasting absolutely *indecent* (the epithet of choice at Georg Rosenberg) . . .

Aside from the water, the heating system was the only other notable break in the otherwise perfect façade of self-control the asylum showed its patients . . . the thermostat was usually broken. Whether it was sunny out or freezing cold, the temperatures indoors were so *indecently* hot that some of the patients periodically banded together to make a joint complaint to one of the nurses. They asked: Are you trying to roast us to death?

But no, no one was trying to roast them to death.

2

But Mylia had been called to the Director's office; her son had been born two weeks before and she still hadn't been allowed to see him.

Doctor Gomperz said, "I hereby notify you that Theodor Busbeck, your husband, has filed for divorce. He asked me to tell you that he wishes you the best, but never wants to see you again."

One way of fighting off loneliness in the asylum was to remind yourself that you were under constant surveillance: it was almost a comfort to feel the heat of so many eyes on your back, and after a while you started to wonder how you ever did without them. True, not everyone was so well socialized: some of the more independent patients cursed at the nurses whenever their glances lingered a little too long . . . and true, whenever more than two patients got together in the common room, they almost always started talking about how many enemies they had at Georg Rosenberg—but we needn't assume, based on these facts, that the atmosphere in the asylum was predominantly one of hostility . . . let us simply observe that a patient like Gada, for example, who'd only just arrived, was already telling his friends *we are engaged on every front*, as though the asylum held enough rival nations to stage a world war . . . and likewise note how many patients spent their free time drawing up what might be called "tactical stratagems": planning the movements of their soldiers and spies (that is, patients, nurses, and doctors) from room to room, redoubt to redoubt, along with numerous and bizarre new implements of war . . . confusing quotidian events like laundry duty with massive, annihilating offensives.

What Mylia paid the most attention to was the way Doctor Gomperz was leading their conversation; it was Gomperz who initiated or dismissed a given exchange, it was Gomperz who decided when they might raise their voices a little . . . and when, on the contrary, they must lower them.

"Have you noticed this painting?" Gomperz asked to Mylia. "It was donated to the institution by the artist himself. He spent some time here, as a patient—and he gave us this gift almost seven years after he was discharged. Do you know what this means? He remembered his time here fondly! People like living here, Mylia."

The surface of the painting dulled in the shadow of Gomperz's arm—as though someone were holding an opaque glass in front of the canvas, dulling its colors.

"The painting is dirty," Mylia said.

"Please," Gomperz said, "don't be ridiculous."

When the mail came, the war councils interrupted their stratagem-making and stampeded toward the stack of envelopes; when a patient didn't receive any mail, he or she became inordinately bitter and cruel for the rest of the day—behavior that was understood and accepted as normal. The patients at Georg Rosenberg had their own form of morality, but it was morality nonetheless: an upsetting, unstable morality, a transitory and restless morality, its tenets varying from day to day, hour to hour, situation to situation. This morality of the moment, this inflexible and immediate form of ethics—straight as a razor blade—was one of the few things that the men and women who passed through Georg Rosenberg all managed to learn: the razor, Lanz would say—a man obsessed with being occupied at all times—and Stonia the nurse would respond: Why yes, Lanz, of course . . . the razor.

It wasn't an easy lesson to forget. Not the sort of thing that just rolls out of your pocket one day and is gone. The basic principle was this: whatever you're feeling, act it out as clearly as you can—no one can blame you for being happy, and, by the same token, every crime is perfectly justifiable when inspired by being sad.

Mail-call was the ideal proving ground for this elementary morality. A letter made everyone take notice—it made the patients excitable in the extreme. After all, each envelope was like a hand beckoning them back to the world outside . . . back to their old lives. Even when a particular letter happened to concern itself with a patient's future, it always appealed most to his or her memory . . . saying, *remember that you've already been here on the outside! . . .* or, more to the point: *don't forget!* Really, every letter to the Georg Rosenberg Asylum said the same thing: don't forget.

There was a gray wheelbarrow in the garden. It was new and seemed out of place given the patients' disinclination to do any chores, and the fact that there were already several perfectly nice flower beds there. Lanz, however, the one patient who wanted to work, had repeatedly asked for a wheelbarrow . . . and now here it was, weeks after he'd given up hope. Things like that happened sometimes: a present appeared, suddenly, unexpectedly. Gomperz stood by the idea that a good surprise, from time to time, helped keep the rage welling up in all his patients—some more than others, naturally—under control. He used their birthdays as a pacification tool—it helped break up the year, helped keep everyone on their toes. Just when they'd lost track of the date, suddenly, without warning, a day was singled out as "special," and an unexpected object—like a wheelbarrow—materialized in the Georg Rosenberg garden. Happy birthday, Lanz.

3

Godicke's excuse to run yelling through the garden that morning was that he'd seen a bloody stain. Gomperz pressed his face lightly against his office window, then turned to Mylia and said: Don't worry, it's only Godicke.

An important decision had been hijacked from Mylia's life. Yes, they'd stolen her decision and driven it cross-country for days, finally abandoning it in the middle of the road, blocking traffic. Without her decision, she was stuck. Everyone was stuck.

Mylia remembered the hiding place in the garden where she sometimes met Ernst to steal a few kisses. Three trees close together, abundant foliage—so perfect for hiding lovers it seemed they'd been planted precisely for that. The patients called them the Trysting Trees . . . Mylia and Ernst hadn't been the first Georg Rosenberg couple to make use of them.

But yes, an important decision had been hijacked from Mylia; this was a concrete fact, a documented event, an occurrence that had been forced inside, or on top of, her life; it was already too late to complain, too late to consider, too late to think up alternatives: like the filthy iron nail in the wall in Mylia's room, dirtying up the space around it, keeping her up nights—there was no arguing with the nail, but of course *this* nail wasn't in her room but in her body, that's where it belonged, they'd hammered it into Mylia's body, which was the most appropriate place, after all (every object and every event has a proper place, of course, and sometimes those places know better than we do what belongs inside them), since they'd stolen a part of her, a part of her body, stolen it in a room she'd never seen before, in the building next to the Georg Rosenberg Asylum—she'd gone in there and then come back out again with a heavy blanket in exchange for her womb. We have to make sure you don't hide anything else in there! one of the doctors had said.

It was a simple enough medical procedure for the age of technology. She wouldn't be able to have any other children; they had torn that possibility, that decision out of her body. Her womb would never have the chance to say "No more!" on its own. They had decided for it, for her.

Mylia hadn't known what they were going to do to her, and later couldn't understand why she was in so much pain, couldn't understand why she was so tired, couldn't understand the bandages. Many years later, long gone from Georg Rosenberg, in another world, someone finally told Mylia what they'd done . . . Did you actually authorize this? they asked.

Mylia, healthy and strong by that point, said: No.

4

Theodor Busbeck, now wealthy and well regarded in the medical field, paid in advance to ensure that his ex-wife would be comfortable for five more years at the Georg Rosenberg luxury hotel for the mentally ill.

She felt, however, that there was a certain hostility toward her at the institution, which Mylia didn't completely understand. It started at the top, with Dr. Gomperz, but went down through all the ranks of employees, becoming especially vicious in the person of certain nurses who, seeing how their boss always acted around her, felt they'd received his tacit seal of approval, and thus formulated a regimen of petty, course cruelties for Mylia's benefit, without fear of reprimand—a little vacation from the rigorous discipline otherwise practiced by the staff.

"You have no idea how much money he cost us!" Gomperz had told Mylia once. She didn't understand that either.

"The painting isn't dirty, *you're* dirty," Gomperz added.

Mylia raised her chin proudly. The cross she'd always worn around her neck had become her refuge, as though to touch it was to enter a different place, to open the door to a safe-room and shut herself inside. When she felt it between her fingers, she was able to be alone, even if she was surrounded by noisy men and women all tugging at her, trying to keep her from "going." But she "went." She "disappeared" from the room. Even if her physical form was still taking up space. The others left her alone then, ignored her, the same way you would leave a piece of furniture alone, something that isn't likely to answer you back.

Wisliz, the man who insisted on telling people he'd swallowed a nail, spoke very slowly, like many people in the asylum; he, like them, seemed to have invented a new language, using the same vocabulary and grammar as before, but more drawn out, an endless string of verbiage, no word given enough space to unfold—its last syllable not yet out, not yet made explicit, before the following word was already pushing itself into the air, consuming its predecessor; the beginning of each word thus melting into the end of the previous—as though it had other, deeper physiological origins . . . a throwback to the birth of intelligible speech.

Yes, Wisliz spoke very slowly, and he constantly drank tea—just like the women patients—trying to dissolve the nail he claimed was in him.

Today, Wisliz picked up an apple—and as soon as it was in his fist, he moved with a new authority: the authority of a living being with two hands who can pick up or put down or juggle a piece of fruit without so much as a second thought. As far as the fruit was concerned, it decided to wait and see where this was heading: with an air of idiotic prudence, it suffered Wisliz to take a bite out of its red flesh and start to chew.

Do you want some apple? Wisliz asked Mylia.

No answer.

They all knew better than to interrupt Mylia when she was "seeing souls." Sometimes she came out of "that place" cursing a blue streak or trying to smash someone's nose in. Besides, it's rude to interrupt a private conversation.

So, today, Mylia sat smiling next to Wisliz, and he smiled too, even though he knew she couldn't see him. That apple was going to be all for him, and that was good enough: Wisliz was happy.

5

One form of therapy encouraged contact with water, a medium often considered calming in the face of certain forms of aggression. Here are the men sitting and smoking in the Georg Rosenberg garden while the women are gathered around a long basin of water, dipping their hands and talking about their favorite sexual positions and gossiping about some of their fellow patients' penises. Thinka, a black woman, who ordinarily prides herself on speaking only in long, outrageously complicated sentences that seem to go on forever, suddenly starts making fun Mylia—rather concisely—and the fact that they took away her son.

She shouts: Ernst is the father! Ernst is the father!

At night, Thinka likes to scare people; she thinks she's invisible in the dark and can sneak up on you without your knowing; she laughs very loudly at every opportunity; she mentions a military hospital she once stayed at where the bed linen was almost as thick as walls—in case of explosions, she explains.

Thinka is an educated woman; she quickly becomes one of the most influential patients; she's strong and has long, fat arms and likes to touch people; her hands take their time on your body; she's always feeling someone up or leaning on them; now she's hanging onto Mylia from behind like a big dark backpack; she kisses her head, her hair; but sometimes too she makes fun of how helpless Mylia is: You weren't cut out to be a mother, Thinka says—without any warning, without so much as an unkind look. It's not calculated, premeditated vindictiveness—it's instinctive, a power display, between one woman and another: a way to keep Mylia in her place.

Thinka says what she says and then says more along the same lines, expanding on her theme: They took him away from you because you weren't cut out to be a mother!

6

Mylia tries to break the glass, but only hurts herself. Witold—who has been at Georg Rosenberg for ten years—says:

"And if you can't feel your soul, break the glass with your soul."

Mylia spits at him, but it doesn't quite work, her saliva stays under her tongue. Witold laughs as she drools. She cleans herself off with the cuff of her sleeve.

Count your fingers, how many are there?

Five, Mylia answers.

See? Witold says. You still have your whole hand.

No, my hand is missing, Mylia insists.

She tries to punch the glass again. Two men grab her.

Mylia can't move her arms, the men won't let her; she opens and closes her right hand dozens of times.

Chapter XXIII
Ernst, Mylia, Hinnerk, Hanna, Theodor

1

They managed to escape from Georg Rosenberg once. The two of them: Ernst and Mylia. They ran through the streets like it was a new world. Life was unrecognizable to them. The men and women they met seemed to be messengers: do you have a letter for us? they wanted to ask. The people in this world dressed as strangely as Ernst walked, but his handicap didn't even raise an eyebrow: everyone was on their way to work, and the morning rush dilutes any amount of strangeness to nearly nothing; running late, people could walk past a dragon without noticing: good morning, they'd say, distractedly, to the monster.

Mylia and Ernst were happy to be anonymous in the midst of such confusion; they were reassured that their escape hadn't really disturbed anything. They weren't all that crazy or all that sick: the city wasn't paying them the least bit of attention.

They smiled at one another while seated in a café. They were in the world, and no one had noticed them: happiness. Mylia leaned across the table and gave Ernst a kiss on the mouth. Just a couple of sweethearts, we're a couple, Mylia thought, and was happy. A couple exchanging a simple kiss in a café.

We're in love, Ernst said to the waiter, who smiled.

Ernst was picking out the bite of cake that he would swallow next. Mylia was whispering something in his ear. A smile here and there. Happy. The café's open door let in an unpleasant chill, but this only amused the sweethearts. How long had it been since they'd had to worry about the temperature outside?

They felt as though they'd gone back to nature. As though, instead of that noisy and smoky café, in the heart of the city, surrounded by the noise of cars, they were actually in the countryside, on some isolated plain.

Mylia sneezed. Ernst offered to switch places with her, so that he would be closer to the door. She declined: It's perfect, she said. Then she sneezed again.

After finishing her own piece of cake, Mylia said:

"The child turns two today."

Ernst realized now how Mylia had picked out the date for their escape.

May 25th? Ernst asked.

May 25th, Mylia answered.

2

Now it was ten years later—or, to be precise, ten years and four days later: May 29th. Four-thirty in the morning. A man by the name of Hinnerk was walking away from a dark little side street. Behind him was the body of a boy: Kaas Busbeck.

Hinnerk needed to find Hanna, urgently. The frustration that had driven him out of his house hadn't been satisfied by his brief encounter with Kaas. This night felt decisive to him, essential to his minimal understanding of the world. He felt like he was researching his own life: Hinnerk still didn't know his own strength, still didn't really know what he was capable of—but tonight it was impossible to respond to life in any way but aggressively, without hesitation, always moving forward. He'd already left one body in his wake, but Hinerk didn't feel like someone walking the streets after having committed a crime—he felt like someone walking the streets after having run into a friend.

He was still breathing hard; the quick fight with the boy had left Hinnerk with a distant but measurable fatigue. He'd never been able to believe in his own strength. He found the ease with which he'd done everything quite odd.

Hinnerk was going to Klirk Purch Street, in the center of the city, where Hanna would certainly be looking for customers, or they would be looking for her. His life fit into Hanna's like a boat in a harbor. Her moorings provided him with a minimum of stability, a point of contact, something he could lean on that wouldn't let him fall. Hanna was his link to the world, to the city, his link to other living beings. There was no underestimating the value of having a person you could talk to once in a while. Hinnerk was well aware that having Hanna in his life helped him keep the greater part of his hostility and violence in check . . . because it was always in him, that violent energy, ready to act.

Tonight, however, it was clear to Hinnerk that this "greater part," the submerged part of him, was going to come to light . . . *his full appetite* would finally be visible. He almost wanted to say *You ain't heard nothin' yet*, like someone who'd received an ovation for what was only his first song—*after all*, he thought, with a criminal kind of modesty, *he was only a kid, I'm capable of so much more . . .*

Feeling the weight of the gun stuck in his waistband, a gun that he hadn't even needed with the boy (whose name he would never know), Hinnerk arrived at Klirk Purch Street and saw Hanna standing next to a man. It was Theodor Busbeck.

Hinnerk walked over to them, smiling, friendly.

1

But on that particular May 25th, the second birthday of Kaas Busbeck, son of Mylia and Ernst Spengler—though officially registered as the son of Dr. and Mrs. Theodor Busbeck, and currently residing with his father—the couple who'd escaped from Georg Rosenberg that morning did not get to see the birthday boy, despite making several attempts.

Theodor Busbeck's house was guarded by a majordomo. No one got in or out without this man's consent. And if the couple had been hoping to catch a glimpse of the boy from a distance, this was equally futile: there wasn't a sign of him, or indeed of anyone, though certain clues as to his presence were hidden nearby—the most obvious being a small toy abandoned in the backyard, which Mylia found after scaling the wall.

Ernst wasn't the type to let himself get agitated, to do anything rude or aggressive, but on this occasion he wasn't able to restrain himself: he went up to the majordomo, who was at Theodor's front door, keeping an eye on the couple—the man who'd simply shrugged at their request to speak to Dr. Busbeck—and clumsily pushed him.

Ernst's so-called attack was sabotaged not only by his general lack of coordination, but also by what you might call a *condition of incompetence* that he'd acquired during his time at Georg Rosenberg: the physical therapy they offered there wasn't focused, naturally, on building strength, since strength is disruptive, but on consistency of pressure, on equilibrium—his muscles, in fact, had been tamed, made into daydreamers: contemplative, patient. Thus, against his will, if Ernst wanted to grab hold of something, he found it wasn't so easy to let go again, and if he wanted to push something, he didn't press and then release, but kept pushing, regrouping, and then pushing again.

The majordomo, however, had a single efficient response to Ernst's flurry of pokes and prods: he reached out and shoved the escapee, which was more than Ernst's legs could handle. Mylia helped him to get up again, but when he was on his feet, Ernst insisted on going back to the door, where the majordomo greeted him with a punch. Ernst fell to the ground with blood on his face.

He began to cry.

2

The first time that Mylia saw her son, he was already four years old, and Theodor Busbeck was present.

Theodor said, "Kaas, get up. This is your mother."

But the boy wouldn't get up. He was rolling around on the floor, up to his father and back, laughing.

Mylia had made some progress. This meant, in essence, that the peculiar energy she'd once exhibited, and which had caused so many problems, had now been cut away—or perhaps simply redirected, hidden somewhere in her body: somewhere she couldn't reach. Action terrified her now. Some days, a closed door was enough to stop her dead. It was risible to think that she, as a human being, had any sort of power to influence the world around her—no, the world was more resilient than Mylia, stronger and more maneuverable; the least thing could topple her, whereas the world . . . there was no fighting it. It was as though the objects that populated her life had all grown to enormous size . . . the littlest bottle seemed gargantuan; how could Mylia hope to pick it up? But this didn't mean Mylia herself had shrunk . . . no, her body too—the one object she couldn't ignore—had also become gigantic, heavy, slow . . . no wonder she could hardly move.

Speaking of bodies, Mylia had once found some dirty magazines wrapped in brown paper in Ernst's room. Everyone knew that the Georg Rosenberg men circulated that kind of thing among themselves, but the women never got to see any of it . . . the exception being Vana, the patient who went around squeezing men between the legs, and who had the filthiest mouth in the asylum.

Still, Mylia was surprised to find out that her boyfriend was the same as the other men—that he had hidden two dirty magazines in his room, all wrapped up like jewels. She sat then for several minutes staring at those pictures—variously sized penises penetrating the vaginas, anuses, and mouths of women staring shamelessly back at the camera . . . it was another world to her. Other women.

Even the nurses knew those magazines were making the rounds at Georg Rosenberg. Since the board hadn't made an explicit ruling on the subject, however, the staff did its best to ignore the problem—only confiscating an issue if a patient was bold enough to show it around in public.

"Kaas, get up. This is your mother."

But despite Theodor's insistence, Kaas barely even looked at Mylia during their first visit: she didn't mean a thing to him, this woman with her glazed expression, her head nodding back and forth, keeping a steady rhythm. If Kaas had known better, he would have said: That's a look of ignorance—the look of a woman who doesn't understand and doesn't care to try. Mylia had only left Georg Rosenberg a week before; this was her second attempt at life on the outside. Her eyes were dull, feeble—and her stare so limp it seemed you'd need to take it by the hand and guide it manually if you wanted her to *see*.

A murky kind of observation, perhaps, but hear me out: there was, at that moment, a measurable difference between the way that Dr. Theodor Busbeck looked at things—his glance snaking quickly out and as quickly disappearing, like mental measuring tape—and the look of this woman he'd identified as Kaas's mother: slow, almost static. Theodor himself had been taught by his father, Thomas Busbeck, that you could always tell how smart someone was by how quickly they moved their eyes. Thomas had said: If we could calculate the rate at which our eyes move over things, taking them in, and then could work out our average eye-speed for an entire year, we would have something very close to a numerical approximation of a person's intelligence—and it would be enough to give us a rather precise idea of that individual's overall value. Really, you can size someone up in just a few seconds if you pay attention—even if he doesn't say a word. What people say doesn't matter . . . maybe they have a good memory. No, said old Thomas Busbeck, if you want to choose a collaborator, close your ears and pay attention to the man's eyes, the way they move, the way they dart toward or away from things, how they size an object up, how they're drawn into it, how they move on or else decide to linger. Our eyes and our minds take the same path through the world . . .

"Kaas," Mylia called, but he didn't pay attention.

"Kaas Busbeck!" Theodor said firmly. "This is your mother."

And the little boy just answered, "No."

Chapter XXV

Hanna, Hinnerk, Theodor, Mylia, Gothjens

1

Hanna was relieved to see Hinnerk, though perhaps less than pleased to find herself in the unusual position of seeing her customer—Theodor—come face to face with her "pimp" (if Hinnerk qualified as such).

Having learned from his father that a famous man's vices should never be kept secret, lest they be used to blackmail him, Theodor had resolved years ago to speak as freely about his "visits to women" as he would about any other subject; he walked the red-light district unashamed and even used his real name when he did so; thus, without hesitation, he offered his hand to Hinnerk and introduced himself as if it were the most natural thing in the world:

"Theodor Busbeck."

There was something unsettling in the name, which sounded vaguely familiar to Hinnerk. He shook the hand of the man who—indirectly—was on the verge of giving him money.

For Hanna, even this short exchange was already too much; she positioned herself between the two men; we'll talk later, she said to Hinnerk, smiling, I need to attend to this gentleman. Theodor said good-bye to the man with the truly "original" bags under his eyes and followed Hanna, whose posterior, he found, undulating as she walked, aroused him with an uncommon intensity.

Hinnerk had only taken a few steps in the opposite direction before it came to him. He thought of the little crippled boy, and, still walking, murmured *Busbeaaak*.

Meanwhile, his feet seemed to have minds of their own, and they were taking him to the church.

2

"Much as you might want it to, your body will never be able to forget its stay at Georg Rosenberg."

Mylia was lying in a bed. This was after she'd first felt the pain in her lower abdomen. She was explaining to the doctor that during her internment, they'd operated on her to keep her from having more children.

Without your consent?" the doctor asked.

"Without my consent," Mylia said.

The gynecologist was an old man: Dr. Gothjens. He sat down and then stood up again, slowly. His voice sounded rigid, tense.

"No doctor can do that without a woman's consent."

"Nobody asked me anything," Mylia said. "Maybe I signed something, but if I did, I was in no condition to do so. I don't remember it."

Dr. Gothjens had already made his diagnosis: the operation at the asylum—to "cut out the possibility of more children," as Mylia put it—hadn't gone well. It achieved its goal—Mylia was sterile—but it had done some damage in the process. She would have to be operated on again. "There's something wrong in there," Gothjens said. "You're healing wrong. We hope this operation can help."

Mylia went back a week later for what would be her first voluntary operation. Three more would follow over the next few years. Until, finally, the doctor, having noted the deterioration of her condition, told her that nothing more could be done . . . she would live two more years, at most. More than that would be a miracle. In his words, she needed to *seek spiritual comfort now, not medicine.*

Mylia remembered her ex-husband's theories. She recognized them coming out of Gothjens's mouth. The spirit, the search for God. The third category of health. When the physical fails.

That same afternoon, she found herself repeating a strange, almost heretical phrase for the first time . . . words that seemed, in retrospect, to characterize her predicament—both a declaration of war and a despairing prophecy:

If I forget thee, O Georg Rosenberg, let my right hand wither.

Chapter XXVI
Ernst

1

Wearing a jacket that was too tight or perhaps even a whole size too small for him, Ernst Spengler used to listen to people talking on the street and try to make sense of their words without tuning in to any one conversation in particular—joining something that a man with a tie was saying to a colleague to whatever a nearby adolescent was saying to two friends. Ernst wanted to keep himself from getting too interested in the details of these individual lives; he wanted to link or weave the entire city's conversations together, so that it would seem to speak with a single voice, seem to speak a simple command, *like a sergeant during wartime*, he thought.

He saw what seemed to be a group of adults playing some kind of game in the distance. As he got closer he decided it was a bunch of dark-faced men moving pots of earth out of a building and onto a pickup truck. When he was closer still he saw a man dressed in black standing by the building: a doorman, obviously, there to offer his expertise. At last the situation had come into focus for Ernst. Someone had died. Two men had arrived in a hearse with an empty coffin. The dead man or woman had lived in one of the apartments in this building. The coffin men had to make sure they had the right address. Solicitous and respectful, the doorman had opened his door as wide as possible so as to allow the coffin and its bearers room to maneuver; an old man, one of the building's residents, had likewise pulled a huge public trash can out of their way, so that they wouldn't bump their elbows going in or coming out.

Ernst had been released from the Georg Rosenberg Asylum several years ago—and today, somewhere in a classier part of the city, his son, whom no one recognized as such, was celebrating his birthday. It was May 25th, a date Ernst would never forget . . . the date of his first escape with Mylia.

Once, on a very busy street, he'd run into an old "associate" from Georg Rosenberg; it was like stepping on a thorn . . . a little obscenity fate had thrown in his path. Ernst hadn't changed for the better, really; he was still just a completely ordinary man, without any noteworthy qualities . . . as long as he was standing still, you could hardly even tell there was anything wrong with him (as opposed to *some* people), but that wasn't much consolation . . . there wasn't a single *positive* thing about him, he knew, that made up for his shortcomings: no artistic ability, no exceptional talent that had emerged—after his leaving the hospital—allowing him to make a triumphant return to human society; his life remained at a steady altitude, and for someone who'd been confined to Georg Rosenberg for so long, this wasn't enough. All the ex-patients demanded something more from their freedom, consciously or not: they wanted a strong, positive change in their lives, some unexpected novelty—even just a woman, for instance, or having a kid . . . some innovation that would make their waiting, their disappointment, the fact that *nothing was happening* bearable.

But . . . since nothing had changed, since nothing had emerged in Ernst Spengler's life that might serve as compensation for his lack of progress, he became uneasy—ferociously so—in the presence of people who'd known him *back then*. Seeing them was nothing more than having his nose rubbed in the evidence of his own, ongoing failure: *You suffered so much, and for what? You barely even have a normal life* . . . Ernst could see them thinking it . . .

Yes, life for Ernst Spengler was really only tolerable when his social interactions were limited to people he'd met after his release, to people in his new life, people who didn't know where he'd been, who didn't know how he'd suffered—because with them, he didn't need to make any existential excuses . . . it was enough for him to be healthy, relatively whole, and alive.

Ernst spent hours walking around the city, making up stories, imagining relationships, connections, friendships between the strangers he saw on the street; he was trying to relearn how to relate to normal people again—and not just normal people, but normal life, normal days: days that just sit there waiting for a human being to decide how to fill them; exactly the opposite of life in the asylum, where he'd been trained for years to sit and accept the regimen that had been decided for him, to follow other people's rules, to fit into other people's schedules. At Georg Rosenberg, each day dawned having already been prepared: engineered, you might say—not in the sense of "constructed," but *genetically*: as though all disturbances and exaggerations had been bred out of life, leaving nothing but a simple and self-explanatory daily routine . . .

Needless to say, this wasn't the only way Georg Rosenberg had left its mark on Ernst; even during his years of supposed freedom, when his illness was dormant, he knew the asylum had sent him back incomplete: his head was safe territory now—for himself as well as for others—but he found it terribly hard to concentrate; the terrain in there was too muddy, thanks to his years away; everything he built collapsed just as quickly; the dams and dikes he tried to erect were insubstantial; his thoughts were always in flux, running together, forming unpredictable, even paralyzing, floods of undifferentiated matter: he could hardly tell one idea from another, could hardly make a single decision . . .

Sometimes, when he cut himself a piece of cake, Ernst Spengler had an absurd and satisfying thought: *Look!* he told himself. *You've managed to separate one thing from another . . .*

2

Ernst couldn't even hope for a reunion with Mylia. Outside of the asylum, it would be catastrophic. Their relationship ended naturally after one of them had left the hospital; that had been many years ago now, and they'd both understood that the world inside and the world outside Georg Rosenberg were like two separate languages—without a single phoneme in common. Nothing meant the same thing in the asylum as it did on the streets; there was no hope of communicating. With both Ernst and Mylia discharged, they'd each forgotten that old language; they might as well have been in a different country; might as well have been different people, using new expressions and following new routines: people who'd never seen each other before, living entirely new lives. Someone had hidden them away for a time, that's all, shut them up in a cul-de-sac, keeping them out of circulation, isolating them from the general population—and that cul-de-sac was called Georg Rosenberg.

"Gomperz, the Director, hid us away," Ernst thought. "Like he was jealous: he didn't want to share us with anyone else in the city. Or like we were diseased: he didn't want anyone else to catch what we had . . . didn't want to see the city decimated by our plague."

But no, there was no plague. They were just crazy.

"That's right. I didn't have a contagious disease," Ernst remembered. "My head wasn't right. That's all."

With each passing week, now removed from life at Georg Rosenberg, Ernst grew more and more resentful of the way he'd been treated. What had then seemed like the only solution—those methods, that discipline (he'd even praised them while he was still a patient)—seemed completely inadequate and even brutal now that Ernst was free to walk the streets among normal men and women. Dr. Gomperz, whom Ernst and all of the institute's "guests" had viewed with such enormous respect—while naturally keeping him at a safe emotional distance—was gradually becoming rather intimidating in his mind, something out of a childhood nightmare: hounding him, hunting him. There's nothing so terrifying to a child as simply *a man chasing after you*—even though, by light of day, such a figure can't really compete with the other, more fabulous monsters that might visit you in your sleep. The thing is, when you hear a fairy tale about someone being hunted, you can't help but feel that this *chase* is directed at you personally, that there's a man on *your* trail hunting *you* and you alone; he's marked you somewhere with an invisible mark and won't ever give up; and if there's anything more horrible than knowing he might catch up with you at any moment, it's the possibility that he never will—that he'll be chasing and chasing you forever. (Ernst had very clear memories of one particular fairy tale he'd heard, where a boy, instead of continuing to run, turned around and faced his persecutor, saying: Here I am, you don't need to run after me anymore—just take me.)

While he'd never been aware of the full extent to which Gomperz had been *pursuing* him at the asylum, after the birth of Mylia's child—a pursuit that never violated the letter of Georg Rosenberg law, but that was real, honest, pure, and malicious persecution nonetheless, with Ernst having indeed been marked with the invisible mark of the eternal victim—and while he was even less aware of the increasingly aggressive surveillance Mylia had been subjected to in the years following all these events: son, divorce, etc.; on the contrary, accepting all the veiled hostility directed at himself or at Mylia as though it were a natural extension of the therapeutic method at the reputable Georg Rosenberg Asylum; even characterizing it as compassionate ("They're helping me!")—Ernst, finally, years after leaving, now distanced at last from all the people (including Mylia) who had interfered with his life, began to see Dr. Gomperz's behavior, and that of the other employees, a little differently. They hadn't helped him (he'd come away with nothing); they hadn't recovered anything he'd lost (that *something*, for instance, that he'd had before he was committed) . . . they'd just been earning their pay, that's all . . . and perhaps what they'd been paid to do was more than a little sinister . . .

Yes, it was growing clearer and clearer in hindsight—coming into focus. Ernst had been punished for the "incident" with Mylia. His tormentor, the person who had made his life a waking nightmare for years and years, was the director of Georg Rosenberg, Dr. Gomperz. That son of a bitch.

3

Today, May 28th, three days after having looked at his calendar and said, My son turns twelve today and has a name that isn't mine, Ernst Spengler, unable to tolerate his growing frustration with the "normal" life he'd made—his so-called freedom in no way a sufficient compensation for the *absence* that had taken up residence in him so long ago, for all the abuse he'd suffered—decided to follow the example of the boy in the fairy tale: the only way to conquer your fear of being chased is to stop running, turn around, and face your persecutor. Only then could Ernst think about finding his son, talking to him, explaining things to him . . . Kaas.

So, this morning, after having a leisurely breakfast in his small attic room, where, thanks to his family's kindness, he'd been living for the last several years, Ernst Spengler headed down the stairs and, once on the street, proceeded at a likewise leisurely pace toward Georg Rosenberg. He needed to speak with the man who was still chasing him, every night, in his dreams: Dr. Gomperz Rulrich.

Chapter XXVII
Theodor

1

Morning on May 28th. Kaas Busbeck, twelve years old today, goes off to school as per usual: his "special" and extremely expensive school, meant to help him improve his speech and muscular control.

On another street in the same city, Ernst Spengler, Kaas's real (but not official) father, heads toward the Georg Rosenberg Asylum, which he hasn't seen in several years—he's even avoided the area surrounding it.

Little Kaas Busbeck walks into school and is well received, as usual. He's a handicapped child and, thus, every relatively fit human adult in his vicinity treats him with compassion and respect—though it may be that at least some of this treatment is due to his father: Theodor Busbeck, who, following in his own father's footsteps, had just been named "Man of the Year," after finally publishing the research that had occupied him for decades: five thick volumes of over eight hundred pages each, published simultaneously, according to their author's explicit instructions. For months, all the magazines—even non-specialty ones—had been featuring reviews, commentary, and analyses of the results obtained from Theodor Busbeck's research. The first four volumes consisted almost exclusively of an impressive block of facts and figures tallying up the victims of all the massacres through-out recorded history. Busbeck's introduction stated the parameters of his study: "I ignored warfare," he wrote. "The confrontation between one force and another force, no matter how unequal, is irrelevant to this work, which focuses on those occasions when Force confronted only weakness"—Busbeck defining "Force" as "matter charged with an inherent, though undirected, energy," and "incapable of acting upon or endangering similarly charged matter (another Force)."

Thus, Dr. Busbeck went on to explain, Force could only be delin-eated relative to neighboring, *uncharged* matter: strength was strength only when confronted by weakness.

Taken in these terms, a "weak" population, with no possibility of resisting or even threatening an invading army, should not be consid-ered "innocent victims," since the question is not one of innocence on one side and evil on the other: Horror, as Theodor saw it, was a matter of *possibility*, not of will or desire. A "weak" population could—in less than a century—become a Force itself: either growing stronger than it had been when last attacked, or simply finding itself near a popula-tion even less capable of defending itself. Busbeck stressed that his research had demonstrated that there was no such thing as a country or people somehow "marked" for suffering, nor indeed any nations gifted with a particular genius for *making* them suffer. "Certainly," Busbeck added, "if you pick out a single moment in history, a specific year, and analyze it out of the context of the whole, you will detect an imbalance in the suffering initiated by or embodied by a particular population . . ." (Busbeck tried to keep his terminology as neutral as possible: he preferred "population enacting suffering" to "butch-ers," preferred "population embodying suffering" to "victims.") But this very imbalance, which even a less comprehensive analysis than

Busbeck's could detect—and which, generally speaking, history acted to correct, over time—indicated to Theodor "that history still hasn't ended"; that, in fact, "the History of Terror is only in its infancy . . . In the coming centuries, we will all get our turn to be massacred. Several billion deaths are, without a doubt, just over the horizon."

2

This was the element of Busbeck's research that went on to cause the most commotion in intellectual circles: his hypothesis that history would cycle on and on until "Group A: Enactors of Suffering" and "Group A^1: Embodiers of Suffering" were balanced "to an identical number of individuals massacred on either side." When this balance was achieved—absolute parity of violence received and executed—life as we've known it would simply cease. Humanity would be over.

This theory had direct, practical consequences; in particular, Busbeck's projection, in the final volume of his work—after having presented exhaustive evidence, over the previous installments, as to who had suffered most and when—of the *massacres to come*. The climax to Busbeck's book ("a brutal coup de grace," as some reviewers put it; or else, "an unnecessary clarification of an already dubious point," to quote the opposition) was a table listing all the nations that would, in the coming centuries, "almost certainly be the target of massacres," and, likewise, the nations that would be responsible for "massacring defenseless populations." He even went so far as to indicate projected death tolls.

The only countries that emerged from this indictment more or less unscathed were those that hadn't recently (over the last few centuries) been the subject or object of any especially notable massacres. The majority, however, were always "in the thick of things," and it wasn't long before Busbeck's work had ignited a bit of a scandal—not so much in the field of mental health, to which Busbeck still nominally belonged, but *sociologically.* What nation on earth would stand idly by as a foreigner calmly published a tidy little table with its name in clear, unambiguous letters, announcing to the world that such-and-such a people would, sooner or later, either perpetrate some unspeakable horror, or else find it visited upon them? Neither option was particularly attractive.

Predictably, then, Busbeck's study met with the most hostility from those scientists hailing from whatever nations had been given the most attention on his terrible table. The interesting thing was—and Theodor often reflected on this in later years—that the reactions he received from those populations prophesied to become "Enactors of Suffering" were just as violent as those that came from populations listed as future "Embodiers." Apparently it was just as offensive to be considered a "future oppressor" as a "future victim"; psychologically speaking, this would seem to indicate that the panic caused by the prospect of either likelihood was basically identical—each of the two basic states of humanity (victim or oppressor) carried with it an identical sense of shame (stemming from some obscure physiological origin, no doubt); another way in which the function of horror was, thought Busbeck, entirely symmetrical.

Yes, the world was a conflict between positive and negative charges; it would end when the two charges finally cancelled each other out, when the balance sheets reached a general, universal—but also personal, microcosmic—zero. The end of everything.

Following Theodor's notion that what applies to the history of mankind applies equally well to the individual man, this meant that, theoretically, it was possible for any human being to predict the day he'd die, since that day, "whenever it will be—far or near—is simply the day on which the positive and negative elements of our lives, the debts owed or deserved, cancel each other out, and equal zero."

And yet, despite its being the logical next step in his theory, Theodor excused himself from drawing up any tables reflecting the balance between the *personal* suffering he himself might have caused or received, and thus what his future might hold . . . not because he wasn't perfectly sincere in his belief that one could apply his general and historical conclusions to the life of an individual—his sincerity was almost mystical, in fact: it was more akin to faith—he just wanted, he claimed, to be "surprised."

Speaking of faith, the "zealous" aspect of Busbeck's work hadn't gone unnoticed. One reviewer in particular took a less than scientific tack:

"Dr. Busbeck, you aren't just a scientist—you are also a believer. This is why your theses carry such weight: your methods, already so rigorous, are bolstered at every moment by your faith. We, mere scientists, so little inclined toward the divine, can only respond to you with the best our meager discipline provides . . . and that is why, should we find ourselves at odds, you will always be the winner . . ."

A less sympathetic response appeared a little while later in our country's "paper of record": an op-ed column by a scientist who was fairly well known, if not famous, in his own field—more biology than psychology—and who, it should be said, hailed from one of the countries included on the table. After spilling much ink to refute each of Theodor's theories point for point, he concluded with the following passage:

"Most esteemed Dr. Busbeck—allow me to address you directly for a moment, before setting down my pen. Sir: by publishing this study, by making public these rash conclusions, drawn from your vast—and perhaps even commendable, in that respect—calculations, you have revealed yourself to be, not a scientist, but—and forgive me for saying so—a lunatic.

"As such," the scientist went on—and Theodor knew that everyone in the city had seen this malicious piece of slander—"there's little point in my continuing to waste my time trying to argue with you scientifically. I will content myself by recommending—and you should be familiar with this kind of recommendation, since you've made it so many times yourself—that you commit yourself to the renowned Georg Rosenberg Asylum, which you might recall has already done your family great service.

"There, being tended to by the highly competent staff, you might begin to recover some of your common sense and capacity for reason . . . In time, you might even find that your synapses are again up to the task of doing real scientific work—a capacity whose continuing absence has been confirmed by your publication of this religious nonsense."

3

Since the biologist's conclusions were basically sound, and, moreover, backed up by his own considerable reputation, his attack marked a significant turn in the reception of Busbeck's study, inaugurating a series of new and more vicious sallies by other scientists—who proceeded to dismantle every one of Theodor's methods and assumptions. The great furor that followed the publication of his five volumes—Theodor's life's work—only lasted a few short years; soon they were only referred to, if at all, as the product of a "certain extravagant mind" who had made "obscene and insulting insinuations" about certain races. Our "Man of the Year" was forgotten, even ostracized. Nor would there be a revival of interest in later decades. The first edition of the book never sold out, despite its initial popularity, and subsequent generations were always assured of finding one or another of its five volumes for sale in secondhand shops amid other old, cheap, unwanted texts: how-to manuals for obsolete technology, or cookbooks so out of fashion you couldn't even be certain of identifying the ingredients they named . . . titles the shop-owners themselves referred to as "books whose day has passed."

Two generations after Busbeck, a volume of his research could be purchased for the price of two cups of coffee.

Chapter XXVIII

Kaas, Ernst, Gomperz

1

Morning on May 28th. Kaas Busbeck, twelve years old today, goes off to school as per usual: his "special" and extremely expensive school, meant to help him improve his speech and muscular control.

On another street in the same city, Ernst Spengler, Kaas's real (but not official) father, heads toward the Georg Rosenberg Asylum, which he hasn't seen in several years—he's even avoided the area surrounding it.

Little Kaas Busbeck walks into school, while Ernst—the father he's never met—prepares to see Gomperz, still the director of the institution that used to be his home.

They made Ernst wait at reception for a good long while. The Director knew he was there, he'd already acknowledged it; he'd told his secretary he "had to take care of something. I'll see him after that." Ernst was back sitting and waiting in a room he'd sat and waited in on so many occasions in the past; he looked around, again seeing those images that had made their way into his head so long ago, but which he'd shut out ever since, along with the "negative feelings" they caused. Being here as a visitor and not as a patient allowed him to see each detail differently.

Certain objects were exactly where Ernst remembered them—when he saw that an ashtray, which he'd first "met" more than ten years ago, was resting in precisely the same position on precisely the same piece of furniture, he had the uncanny feeling that it was a magic trick intended for his benefit: that the Georg Rosenberg, and particularly its Director, had somehow frozen time. As a matter of fact, being "frozen" was what living at the asylum had felt like . . . yes, they had frozen him in place long enough for him to return to "the world" back in step with its other inhabitants. Staring now at that eternal ashtray, Ernst understood clearly that it had always been a question of velocity. Now he was older, of course, and out in the world—but it wasn't the same world he'd left. Back when he was strong, when he'd moved too fast for the world, they'd taken him away from other human beings—and as soon he began to weaken, they threw him back out into life. The world grew strong as Ernst grew weak.

He hadn't seen Mylia since. One of the "positive" reasons he'd decided to go back to Georg Rosenberg—to that "negative" place—was to ask the *esteemed* Dr. Gomperz for her address. He wanted to get back in touch with Mylia, to know if she ever saw their son; to know, finally, if it might be possible for him, Ernst Spengler—a man who, legally, had no rights as far as little Kaas Busbeck—to see the boy too, if only for a few hours. This had become more and more important to Ernst over recent months, almost an obsession: to see his son!

Was Kaas all right? Was he healthy? It was horrible not to know. And Ernst refused to let himself speculate.

Of course, he could have tried to find out about Kaas through Theodor Busbeck, the "eminent researcher," but didn't have the courage. That man had always made Ernst feel panicky and inferior. Mylia, on the other hand . . . surely she'd allow him to see their son . . . maybe even talk to him.

But seeing Mylia again would no doubt be traumatic for both of them. Perhaps even more so than seeing Gomperz again. It would bring back all the days they'd spent together . . . one by one, all the days at Georg Rosenberg.

The Director will see you now.

Chapter XXIX
Ernst, Gomperz, Mylia, Hinnerk

1

"My dear Mr. Ernst Spengler! It's been too long. You look absolutely wonderful. And note that I still remember your name."

Ernst was immediately disgusted with the sight of Gomperz, though the touch of his limp, unnerving hand might have been worse . . . *an insulting hand*, he thought.

"Come in, my dear Mr. Spengler—it's not every day that an old 'student' of mine comes to visit! Come in and sit down. Let's talk a little. I've set aside ten minutes just for you. Forgive me for having made you wait, but as always, we've got a lot of work to do here—as I'm sure you know, our patients need constant care! But, let me tell you, we always have a very few openings for anyone who needs our help . . . That's the best indication of whether we're doing a good job, don't you think? Tell me, do you remember your years here? The occupancy rate was good then too, but now it's even better.

"Ernst Spengler! How I've missed saying your name out loud. Dear Ernst, you know, you were lucky enough to spend time in what was our city's best clinic . . . and now, all these years later—how many, do you think? I can't keep track!—and now, as I was saying, we're *still* the best! I'm so proud of our work here, and I hope you are too."

Gomperz was nervous. Maybe even as nervous as Ernst. All that talking wasn't just a noisy demonstration of authority, wasn't just polite condescension; those words of his had been excreted—yes, excreted—to show Ernst that Gomperz was as sharp as ever, in full possession of faculties, physical and mental. Yes, perhaps his former "student" would see that the Director was a little older, a little more stooped, but he shouldn't be deceived: Gomperz was, as ever, the one in control . . . as much as Ernst, as always, was vulnerable.

"So tell me, Ernst, what brings you back to dear old Georg Rosenberg? Tell me how you've been, what you've been up to. We're very interested in the people who pass through these walls, of course, hearing what they've made of themselves. Our students' successes are proof that we do good work! Yes, we're all just sentimental old grade-school teachers here, Ernst, and believe me when I tell you: I'm very moved to see you again, and to see you looking so good. So please: don't leave me in suspense! What are you doing with yourself?"

Spengler was quiet, then gave a short, circumstantial answer. Then, noting the new tone creeping into his own voice, he said:

"I needed to see you again. I haven't been able to get you out of my mind for years . . ."

Gomperz picked up on Ernst's aggression immediately.

"That's quite normal, my friend. The time you spent here wasn't easy—you had a number of difficulties, and we had to be firm with you. Nothing gets accomplished here without a certain amount of 'rigor.' I do hope you never took any of it personally . . ."

"Above all," Ernst interrupted him, "I'm here because I want Mylia's address."

And then a pause. Gomperz began shuffling the loose papers around on his desk with his fingertips, as he often did when he was about to say something of significance:

"I'm sorry, Ernst, but I can't provide you with confidential information. It goes against our rules."

Ernst tried to maintain eye contact.

"We simply can't give out a former patient's address to another former patient. If you were a blood relative, perhaps . . . but it's irrelevant: we don't have Mylia's current address. I remember her very well, of course, but we've lost touch with her. We don't know what she's doing, and we don't know where she lives."

Again, silence.

"Have you tried asking around? With a name like hers I'd think she'd have trouble hiding."

"I haven't been able to find her."

"I'm very sorry," Gomperz said as he rose from his chair—an unequivocal sign that their meeting was over. "In any event," he continued, "leave your contact information with me. Perhaps, if we manage to track her down ourselves, we'll . . . well, we'll be able to turn a blind eye to some of the board's overcautious regulations . . ."

Instinctively obeying the Director—he regretted it immediately—Ernst dutifully wrote down his address and phone number.

"You must know how important it is for me to find Mylia again," he said.

"Of course, Ernst. Don't worry. I don't have a heart of steel—you don't really know the real me at all! I'll do everything I can to put you two in touch. You can be sure of that."

Ernst was on his way out—but before closing the office door, he turned around and asked, "Do you know the real reason I came to see you?"

Gomperz smiled, his expression softening, taking on the air of "a good listener."

"Do you remember," Ernst went on, "what you used to say to us all the time . . . that a person's mental health wasn't so much concerned with what he *did*, but with what he was *thinking*? Do you remember asking us: *what are you thinking*? Do you remember how much that question terrified us? Well . . . if you were to ask me that question today, now that I feel a little more balanced, do you know what I would say? That in the last few days, what I've been thinking about is killing you. I think I needed to see you to get rid of that desire . . . and, as a matter of fact, I don't have it anymore, it's gone. Director Gomperz, I was watching you very carefully just now, your face, your movements . . . I don't know if you've noticed, but you're an old man now . . . If I didn't recognize you, and I met you on the street, I might even try, despite my weakness, to help you cross the road . . . So I'm going to stop thinking about you, Director. You aren't a monster, you're just an old man. Understand? The boy isn't running anymore. He's looking right at you—and he's happy."

2

Mylia lived on the first floor at 77 Moltke Street. Sitting in an uncomfortable chair, she was thinking about the essential words in her life. *Pain*, she thought, *pain* is an essential word.

She'd already had one operation, then another, four operations in all. And now this—this sound deep in the center of her body. Being sick, she told herself, is a test, a way to teach yourself how to endure pain. Or else: it's a manifestation of your desire to get closer to Almighty God. And churches are closed at night.

Four in the morning on May 29th. Mylia couldn't sleep. The pain was constant, coming from her stomach—or maybe lower. Where exactly was it coming from? Maybe from her womb. The only thing she knew for sure was that it was four in the morning and she hadn't slept a bit. She couldn't close her eyes because she was afraid of dying.

That afternoon she'd received a phone call from Doctor Gomperz. It had been years since she'd last heard his voice. How disgusted she felt, hearing it. The Director of Georg Rosenberg.

"I'm going to give you Ernst Spengler's address and telephone number," he said, after an *affectionate greeting*. "He was here this morning and would really like to talk to you." Gomperz added that he was so happy to hear how well Mylia was doing. He said her voice "sounded strong and healthy."

Mylia wanted to thank him for the fact that she didn't have much longer to live. But she refrained.

She wondered why Gomperz himself had made the call. He could've gotten one of his employees to do it.

It didn't matter. The rest of her day had been ruined. That man's voice stayed in her ear. It sloshed around like some sort of liquid. Mylia kept wiggling her finger around inside to try and get it out. *Motherfucker*, she muttered.

Gomperz's voice opened the floodgates. Mylia found herself thinking of things she'd managed to avoid for years. *You have to eat*, that's what they always told her in the cafeteria, even when she said she wasn't hungry . . . Georg Rosenberg, she remembered the door of the Georg Rosenberg Asylum, and the book that fell on floor, and the slap they gave her because that book, "the most important book," the Bible, was full of staples, *who did this?*, oh, someone had stapled a bunch of the Bible's pages together, they were very thin pages covered with word after holy word, and Mylia just couldn't understand how all those words in a row had all turned out to be holy, what a coincidence that they were all already in one book, yes, the Georg Rosenberg Asylum's Great Book of Staples, and Mylia remembered too how the other patients had laughed when a nurse tried to pry the pages apart again without ripping them—Ecclesiastes, motherfucker! Saint Mark, Saint Luke, Letter to the Romans, First Letter to the Corinthians, absolutely, you cunt, every one of them stapled together! And remember, in Corinthians, how it says, "The last enemy that shall be destroyed is death"? But that wasn't the best part, no, the good bit was: "With what body do they come?"

Mylia was doubled over because of the pain, yes, four in the morning, impossible to sleep: "With what body do they come?"

On Sundays, Dr. Gomperz usually read passages from the Bible to the patients himself: faith keeps one's thoughts correct and thus heals the body. Sacrifice yourself and you will be rewarded, he used to say. "We'll be transformed." First Letter to the Corinthians, 15:51, "Behold, I show you a mystery; We shall not all sleep, but we shall all be changed." Dr. Gomperz with his authoritarian voice. This is still therapy. We shall be changed. Matthew 4:1: "Then was Jesus led up of the spirit into the wilderness to be tempted of the devil. And when he had fasted forty days and forty nights . . ."

"He was hungry," said Mylia.

3

Mylia was already out on the street and had to go to a church—it was an emergency. Ernst's home was practically next door, but she didn't want to run into Ernst Spengler. How many years had it been since they'd last seen each other? I've moved on, she thought. I am in another world, I can't go backwards.

She looked at the piece of paper where she'd written his address and telephone number. Back in the Georg Rosenberg days, Ernst Spengler had been what you might call a pretty face. They'd fallen in love thanks to his face: a woman reads things into a face, Mylia thought, reads a man differently, sees his insides, the skin under his skin, his emotional skin . . . Ernst's chin was narrow and his eyes were square-set, like a general's at war: *commanding eyes*, she'd said. They'd kissed behind the Trysting Trees; they'd gotten too excited, and Mylia had come out with a mark on her neck; Ernst Spengler is a beautiful man, Glori said to her. But Mylia pretended Glori had said Ernst was hideous.

The night was pretty much deserted and Mylia ran into a bum. Surprised, the bum says he doesn't know. A church?

"Arise, and take the young child and his mother, and go into the land of Israel: for they are dead which sought the young child's life." Matthew 2:20.

Do you know if they're all closed at this hour? Churches?

Her shoes flat on the ground. A face again, but not her lover's face: Gomperz's face. They cut her up. Nobody at Georg Rosenberg dies in the spring—don't worry, it's just a routine operation, they said.

She thought of Kaas, her son: he'd turned twelve a few days before. A mother should be able to see her son, her beautiful boy—but, clearly, Kaas wasn't: wasn't a beautiful boy. Oh, his face is all right, like Ernst Spengler's, a beautiful face like his father's, but not the rest of him: that ridiculous limp, his speech—he shouldn't let people make fun of him, he shouldn't walk around in front of them, he should just stay sitting down until he's an adult.

Sometimes she couldn't help but notice how little she cared about her son. Who is he to me? They stole him. Kaas is a pretty name, but he hasn't given me any reason to be proud of him . . .

"The church is closed. Do you have any idea what time it is? It's almost five in the morning. You shouldn't be out here anyway. This is a bad neighborhood at night. It's dangerous."

"I really need to get in . . ." Mylia said.

Come back at eight, the man said.

"Do you know if there are any churches still open?"

4

Mylia was so hungry it took her a moment to separate the pain of her hunger from the pain that the doctors had guaranteed would kill her. Science had said she would die. It would take a miracle . . .

In Matthew, it is written that the Three Wise Men, after having paid homage to the Child, "departed into their own country," but "by another way." After they had seen the Child, they didn't return by the same road.

Mylia walked off to urinate leaning up against a tree. When she came back it was on the other side of the church, to the rear.

She understood then that there, right there, next to the church, her two pains were trying to outdo each other: the pain that would kill her, the bad pain, as she called it, the sickness pain, and, on the other hand, the good pain, the hunger pain, the pain of wanting to eat, a pain that signified life, the pain of existence, as she would say; as though her stomach, even in the dead of night, was the one obvious sign of her humanity . . . and likewise of humanity's ambiguous relationship with the things in the world it still couldn't understand. Yes, she was alive, and this proof of being alive hurt even more, at this moment, in an objective and physical way, than the pain she knew was going to kill her. As if, tonight, it was more important to have a bite of bread than live forever.

Mylia looked around: where can I get something to eat at this time of night?

Now, behind the church, Mylia took out the piece of chalk she had in her purse and wrote, in letters so small they were barely visible: *hunger.*

She felt her stomach throbbing again—with the second, new pain. She lowered her hand, dropping the chalk, and started walking, heading for another street. She was hungry. The pain was becoming unbearable.

Hurrying along, she reminded herself, almost amused, I'm so hungry, I'm not going to die! It's impossible to die when you're this hungry!

The hunger made her feel strangely safe: the pain of hunger was a guarantee, a promise, at least for the time being. The other pain can't sneak up and kill me when *this* pain is so strong! And now that she felt safe, she tried to take her mind off eating. If I eat something, the hunger pain will pass, and then I'll feel the other pain again . . . and that one *can* kill me.

There was a light in the distance now, maybe a café that was already open, with a telephone booth to its right. The hunger pain was worse and worse. I need to eat something soon or I'll die, she told herself—and laughed.

Then she stopped laughing. She took out the piece of paper with Ernst's phone number. She took out a few coins too and put one in the phone's slot. She dialed Ernst's number: it started ringing. No one answered. Four, five, six.

5

Ernst Spengler was alone in his attic apartment with the window open. It was past five in the morning, May 29th. The day before had been too much. Something was troubling Ersnt, something old and sinister. Seeing Gomperz again had dislodged some *dark energy* in him. He wasn't past it yet.

He'd opened the window several minutes before; there was a draft coming into his apartment, moving over his furniture, covering everything with the invisible muck of the world; soon the outside and the inside seemed to have come to an agreement, formed an alliance, the two contraries dissolving into a single space. The chill and menace of the night air didn't have to come in through the window anymore—it was everywhere, there was only *outside*.

Ernst was overexcited. Thoughts and images were rushing into one another at a greater speed than usual—each had hardly formed before another popped up to take its place: his usual cycle having been abridged to the point of near-incomprehensibility. All he was certain of was a mounting sensation of expectation—an invitation to act. The window was just large enough to accommodate a human body, and his body wanted to move, to react to that overwhelmingly seductive egress, seemingly made just for him: a simple invitation for a simple man who, on that night of May 29th, couldn't sleep.

And then the telephone rang. Ernst stopped and that succession of thoughts and images fell away—as though they were physical things, easily dropped. He went to the phone.

It rang again and again: five, six, seven, eight, nine, ten, eleven, twelve, thirteen, fourteen. Ernst answered.

On the other end of the phone someone said, "Ernst—I'm near the church. Hello?"

It was Mylia's voice.

And then there was the sound of a body falling.

6

Ernst is crouching over Mylia—she's just coming to.

Ernst touches her cheek gently with his index finger, by her right eye.

Mylia smiles: the voice has turned into a body. Ernst came by an indirect route.

Mylia thinks: I recognized your hand before I even opened my eyes.

"Your right hand didn't wither. You see mine? It didn't wither either."

Ernst asks Mylia not to speak. He tries to help her up, can't.

"Where have you been?" Mylia wonders.

They embrace. Ernst tries to lift her again. He can't. They hear a voice:

"Do you need help?"

They both turn. It's a man. A man named Hinnerk Obst, who's come from killing a little boy named Kaas—*Kaas Busbeaaak*, as the boy himself had said.

"Yes," Ernst said. "It's my friend, she fainted. Please help us."

1

"She's weak," Ernst said.

"I'll help," Hinnerk said.

Each man took an arm, and together they were able to get Mylia to her feet. With almost all her weight resting on Hinnerk, they helped her to a park bench only a few meters up the street

"Sit down," Hinnerk said. Mylia sat down.

"Thank you," said Ernst. "My leg is weak."

Mylia was tired, but she smiled at Hinnerk.

"Thank you for your help," Ernst said again. "We're fine now, there's no need for you to hang around. We're old friends. We've already caused you enough trouble."

Hinnerk shook his head. It was no problem, he wasn't in a rush. He would stay as long as necessary.

Hinnerk was relieved: his aggression was petering out. *Being able to help someone*—as insignificant as that help was—seemed to have changed something in his body: it was *a deflection of desire.* It pleased him to discover that he could be useful to someone, and the simple, appreciative looks this man and woman were giving him pleased him as well. He was used to people—mainly children—looking at him in fear, or else making fun of the bags under his eyes . . . saying he looked like a killer.

But now, this couple was actually happy to see him . . . or they were, initially. Hinnerk was starting to feel that the man and the woman might want to be alone. They wanted to talk. They were old friends. They didn't know him. It was normal.

Hinnerk had an impulse then that he couldn't quite understand, though it seemed reminiscent of the childish need *to impress* . . . He lifted up his shirt and drew his gun from his pants, saying—not at all aggressively, as though expecting to be praised:

"Look what I've got."

And Ernst and Mylia recoiled.

2

Meanwhile, after Hinnerk had left Klirk Purch Street, heading for the church, Hanna and Dr. Theodor Busbeck had gone up to a hotel room.

The hotel wasn't awful, though Theodor could easily have afforded one of the city's far more elegant—and more discreet—upscale brothels . . . Still, as previously stated, he wasn't the least bit afraid of being seen, nor was he particularly squeamish. He was a divorced man—he didn't have to answer to any woman at home. He had a son and knew how to raise him; the fact that Theodor picked up whores on the street didn't make him a bad father, as far as he was concerned. I'm a man, Theodor thought—and this redundant biological affirmation cancelled out any moral contradictions in his behavior. The dirtiness, the danger he enjoyed on the streets was something that couldn't be replicated in a discreet, high-class brothel. Just like his father, Thomas Busbeck, Theodor couldn't resist the allure of feeling that he'd left his privileged, educated milieu behind—that world of delicate words delicately inserted in all the proper places in each delicate sentence—to enter another one, where men and women showed their ignorance at every moment, spewing obscenities without reserve, using incorrect, folksy grammar, and speaking with accents that branded them as having come from the country, not the city—yes, Theodor found it all terribly exciting. It wasn't just sexual: his investigation into this other world was prompted too by his basic scientific curiosity; it was a consequence of his instincts as a "researcher," as he himself explained to his friends: he was drawn to the foreign, the unfamiliar, to new and unforeseen information. Any researcher worth his salt should be interested in delving into the unknown, Theodor used to say. And you can't discover anything worthwhile without taking a few risks.

Which isn't to say that Theodor didn't have doubts about his nighttime "constitutionals." There was anxiety . . . even fear. He could have been robbed at any moment, after all . . . and men who looked likely to rob him were on every corner. What worried Theodor was that he might, unintentionally, give them an excuse to challenge him: that some kind of misunderstanding might crop up. Theodor wasn't a physical man, he wasn't used to direct physical confrontation, you could tell as much just by looking at him—but he couldn't help himself, couldn't stop visiting this part of town, even though he knew he'd probably get himself killed some day. He wouldn't be the first one.

And now here he was again. Always looking for new women, different women. Tonight his woman was Hanna. She'd captivated him. They'd set a rendezvous. She was forceful, demanding. She gave the orders. She's in front of him, she's unlocking the door to their room, her short skirt leading him inside.

"Come in, Mister."

3

At the same time, by the church, three people—two men, Hinnerk and Ernst, and a woman, Mylia—are laughing and playing with a gun; Mylia's got it now, she likes the weight of it, the shape of its trigger (she's never seen a gun before, she says); *at the same time*, that is, on May 29th, when, in another part of the city, on what we might call a "lively" street, Theodor Busbeck, Mylia's ex-husband, is watching a whore named Hanna strip off her clothes in room number 14 of one of the hotels frequented by the Klirk Purch Street prostitutes.

Theodor was about two meters away, smiling as he undid the buttons of his shirt. Hanna took off her top—and once her bra was off, her breasts fell, flaccid, almost down to her belly.

An unpleasant something or other was creeping up on Theodor Busbeck. Under the bright overhead light of their hotel room, he was finally able to see Hanna clearly: the face that had seemed perfect and young out on the streets now seemed . . . well, not ugly, but certainly plain, and, moreover, quite wrinkled. And those breasts—falling crudely over her torso, nipples almost nonexistent. The woman was old. A few hours earlier she'd looked like she was twenty, but now it was obvious that she could be fifty. She stripped off her skirt and lowered her panties; Theodor, watching, shuddered and took a small, almost imperceptible, step backward. Hanna's pubic area was completely shaved; her wrinkled genitals sat atop the loose flesh of her legs, which crept down her bones like some viscous liquid. And right next to those rude, old, red genitals: a dark stain, an enormous stain, larger than Theodor's hand, a blotch on the inside of her thigh.

Hanna noticed her client looking at "that." She said, "It's a burn," but Theodor didn't even hear her. He was too terrified.

Mylia still has the gun. What fun they're all having. Mylia points the gun at Hinnerk, the man who helped them. She's lost interest in being alone with Ernst. She doesn't want to remember the time she spent at the Georg Rosenberg Asylum. She doesn't want to have any conversations about the past, doesn't want Ernst to ask about their son, doesn't want to think about their son, just wants to stay here playing with this gun until the church opens, playing with the gun that belongs to this nice man with the huge bags under his eyes.

Mylia is increasingly interested in Hinnerk. She's ignoring Ernst, really. She's sorry now; she wishes she hadn't called him. Georg Rosenberg was a long time ago. Her hand hadn't withered, and this just wasn't the right time to talk to Ernst about everything. In fact, it would never be the right time. Mylia wants Ernst to forget all about Kaas. She wants Ernst to stay away from the boy. She is ashamed, she's realized, of Ernst Spengler.

She turns toward the man, toward Hinnerk: so, if I pull the trigger now, it'll shoot? she asks—and she's forgotten her pain, forgotten the pain of her hunger. Hinnerk says no. He laughs, explains how it works: You have to lift this lever first. Hinnerk lifts the lever, Ernst laughs, Mylia points the gun at Hinnerk, so now it'll shoot? she asks. Hinnerk answers yes, and Mylia keeps the gun pointed at Hinnerk's head. "And what if I shoot?" Mylia asks this man whom she feels a little attracted to, in all honesty—a little excited by. "So shoot," Hinnerk says, amused, "go on and shoot!"

Chapter XXXI
Mylia

1

Mylia is forty-eight years old now and is locked up in a cell in a hospital for the criminally insane. She still has a few years of her sentence to serve. According to the doctors, "she should have been dead already" a long time ago, since her condition is, medically, untenable.

But, as her ex-husband had repeated countless times, the third category of health has nothing to do with men or their medicine . . . and this was what Mylia had achieved.

She was alive because there had been a miracle. Yes, *spiritual comfort, not medicine.*

The pain in or near her womb is still there—stronger on some days, weaker on others—but Mylia is alive and has gotten used to the way that the pain helps her remember what they did to her at the Georg Rosenberg Asylum.

"If I should forget thee, O Georg Rosenberg . . ."

But it was impossible for Mylia to forget. My right hand didn't wither, she told herself, caressing her own neck.

In addition to the pain, life in prison—with its rigid schedule—was itself a reminder of the time Mylia had spent in the asylum. Being told when you have to wake up or go to sleep, eating at set times, having to participate in various activities spaced throughout the day to prevent any dead time that might lead to "unpredictable thoughts," meeting here and there with fellow inmates and indulging in a certain "verbal promiscuity," sharing secrets with one prisoner or another as she'd done with her crazy friends at Georg Rosenberg . . . really, the similarities were so striking that it sometimes seemed to Mylia that the Georg Rosenberg years were repeating themselves . . . or else, that she'd been transported into the past. Nothing would really have surprised her, at this point.

Still, there was an important difference: this time, there was no Gomperz.

The prison warden was practically invisible. Mylia had seen him once or twice: he didn't interfere with the prisoners' activities. She immediately liked him. His absence was his most prominent feature. His most likable feature.

She had been convicted of the murder of an adult male by the name of Hinnerk Obst on the night of May 29th of the year . . . etc. She'd shot him in the head.

Whenever anyone asked what she was in for, she always answered exactly the same way: "I was convicted of the murder of an adult male by the name of Hinnerk Obst on the night of May 29th of the year . . . etc."

That same night, her son, Kaas, had been killed in such a gruesome fashion that no one ever had the temerity to give Mylia the news. His murderer was never identified.

Chapter XXXII
Mylia, Ernst, Hinnerk

1

Mylia laughed and lowered the gun. Ernst asked to have it next.

Yes, go on, Hinnerk said.

Ernst lifted the gun. It's heavy, he said.

That's the way they all are, Hinnerk said. During the war, I used to have to carry machine guns that were at least fifty times heavier than that pistol.

You were in the war? Mylia asked.

Yes, Hinnerk answered.

Did you kill people? Mylia asked, increasingly excited by this unique situation, by this nice man, by the pain in her stomach, which had now come back—but was it the hunger pain or the other one?

Of course I killed people, Hinnerk said.

Really? Mylia said.

Of course, Hinnerk said.

And then a roar blew Hinnerk's head off.

Ernst was still holding the gun. The bullet came out, he said.

What did you do, idiot! Mylia says. You killed the man!

Mylia was yelling and yelling. Then Ernst turned and tried to get away as fast as possible. As fast as was possible with his ridiculous right leg.

"You son of a bitch!" Mylia screams.

And then Mylia went quiet. The gun was on the ground, and Ernst was gone.

She looks down and sees the man with the shattered head. Idiot, she says, careless! Ernst, idiot, lunatic!

Mylia tries to think, tries to understand what she should do. People will come soon, someone must have heard, there are no residences around, but somebody must have heard, Mylia thinks. At least in the church. They must have heard in there.

Now she hears noises coming from the church. More noise from the church; but, soon, it's over, no one comes out. What's going on? Mylia wonders. No one's coming?

A lot of time is passing and still no one's shown up. Didn't anyone hear? Maybe they're afraid in there, inside the church, Mylia thinks.

She hasn't moved. Now she bends over, picks up the gun, grabs it, and starts to walk toward the church's front door. It's still night, but there might be a tiny ray of light visible now in the sky. What time is it? Mylia doesn't know.

She's in front of the church door, her arms dangling loosely at her sides, there's some blood on her clothes and a gun in her right hand, pointing at the ground. She can tell now that her usual pain isn't bothering her at all, but her hunger is much, much worse—all she can think about is food, bread, milk. The sun could be rising, and Mylia feels like fainting, but she resists. She can hear noises, finally, coming from inside the church, behind the main door; someone is there, right there on the other side of the door, not even two meters away. Her hunger levels off then; she almost manages to forget it.

The sound of door being unlocked, then it opens very slightly, hardly a crack, Mylia sees eyes staring out at her, fearfully, carefully. She can't take much more—her tense right hand is tight around the gun and she really, really wants to faint. Still the eyes are watching her, and still the door isn't opening any wider. Mylia will have to speak to whomever is on the other side of the church door. She tries to collect herself. She calls up the sternest voice she can manage.

"I killed a man," she says. "*Now* will you let me in?"

FROM THE NOTEBOOKS OF GONÇALO M. TAVARES | 10

GONÇALO M. TAVARES was born in 1970. He has published numerous books since 2001 and has been awarded an impressive number of literary prizes in a very short time, including the Saramago Prize in 2005. He was also awarded the Prêmio Portugal Telecom de Literatura em Língua Portuguesa 2007 for *Jerusalem*. His novels *Learning to Pray in the Age of Technology*, *Klaus Klump: A Man*, and *Joseph Walser's Machine* all comprise sections, along with *Jerusalem*, of a series Tavares calls *The Kingdom*. These titles are all forthcoming in English translation from Dalkey Archive Press.

ANNA KUSHNER is the translator of *The Halfway House* by Guillermo Rosales and *The Autobiography of Fidel Castro* by Norberto Fuentes. She was a finalist for the John Guyon Literary Nonfiction Prize in 2007.

SELECTED DALKEY ARCHIVE PAPERBACKS

PETROS ABATZOGLOU, *What Does Mrs. Freeman Want?*
MICHAL AJVAZ, *The Other City.*
PIERRE ALBERT-BIROT, *Grabinoulor.*
YUZ ALESHKOVSKY, *Kangaroo.*
FELIPE ALFAU, *Chromos.*
 Locos.
IVAN ÂNGELO, *The Celebration.*
 The Tower of Glass.
DAVID ANTIN, *Talking.*
ANTÓNIO LOBO ANTUNES, *Knowledge of Hell.*
ALAIN ARIAS-MISSON, *Theatre of Incest.*
JOHN ASHBERY AND JAMES SCHUYLER, *A Nest of Ninnies.*
HEIMRAD BÄCKER, *transcript.*
DJUNA BARNES, *Ladies Almanack.*
 Ryder.
JOHN BARTH, *LETTERS.*
 Sabbatical.
DONALD BARTHELME, *The King.*
 Paradise.
SVETISLAV BASARA, *Chinese Letter.*
MARK BINELLI, *Sacco and Vanzetti Must Die!*
ANDREI BITOV, *Pushkin House.*
LOUIS PAUL BOON, *Chapel Road.*
 My Little War.
 Summer in Termuren.
ROGER BOYLAN, *Killoyle.*
IGNÁCIO DE LOYOLA BRANDÃO, *Anonymous Celebrity.*
 Teeth under the Sun.
 Zero.
BONNIE BREMSER, *Troia: Mexican Memoirs.*
CHRISTINE BROOKE-ROSE, *Amalgamemnon.*
BRIGID BROPHY, *In Transit.*
MEREDITH BROSNAN, *Mr. Dynamite.*
GERALD L. BRUNS, *Modern Poetry and*
 the Idea of Language.
EVGENY BUNIMOVICH AND J. KATES, EDS.,
 Contemporary Russian Poetry: An Anthology.
GABRIELLE BURTON, *Heartbreak Hotel.*
MICHEL BUTOR, *Degrees.*
 Mobile.
 Portrait of the Artist as a Young Ape.
G. CABRERA INFANTE, *Infante's Inferno.*
 Three Trapped Tigers.
JULIETA CAMPOS, *The Fear of Losing Eurydice.*
ANNE CARSON, *Eros the Bittersweet.*
CAMILO JOSÉ CELA, *Christ versus Arizona.*
 The Family of Pascual Duarte.
 The Hive.
LOUIS-FERDINAND CÉLINE, *Castle to Castle.*
 Conversations with Professor Y.
 London Bridge.
 Normance.
 North.
 Rigadoon.
HUGO CHARTERIS, *The Tide Is Right.*
JEROME CHARYN, *The Tar Baby.*
MARC CHOLODENKO, *Mordechai Schamz.*
EMILY HOLMES COLEMAN, *The Shutter of Snow.*
ROBERT COOVER, *A Night at the Movies.*
STANLEY CRAWFORD, *Log of the S.S. The Mrs Unguentine.*
 Some Instructions to My Wife.
ROBERT CREELEY, *Collected Prose.*
RENÉ CREVEL, *Putting My Foot in It.*
RALPH CUSACK, *Cadenza.*
SUSAN DAITCH, *L.C.*
 Storytown.
NICHOLAS DELBANCO, *The Count of Concord.*
NIGEL DENNIS, *Cards of Identity.*
PETER DIMOCK, *A Short Rhetoric for Leaving the Family.*
ARIEL DORFMAN, *Konfidenz.*
COLEMAN DOWELL, *The Houses of Children.*
 Island People.
 Too Much Flesh and Jabez.
ARKADII DRAGOMOSHCHENKO, *Dust.*
RIKKI DUCORNET, *The Complete Butcher's Tales.*
 The Fountains of Neptune.
 The Jade Cabinet.
 The One Marvelous Thing.
 Phosphor in Dreamland.
 The Stain.
 The Word "Desire."
WILLIAM EASTLAKE, *The Bamboo Bed.*
 Castle Keep.
 Lyric of the Circle Heart.
JEAN ECHENOZ, *Chopin's Move.*
STANLEY ELKIN, *A Bad Man.*
 Boswell: A Modern Comedy.
 Criers and Kibitzers, Kibitzers and Criers.
 The Dick Gibson Show.
 The Franchiser.
 George Mills.
 The Living End.
 The MacGuffin.
 The Magic Kingdom.
 Mrs. Ted Bliss.
 The Rabbi of Lud.
 Van Gogh's Room at Arles.
ANNIE ERNAUX, *Cleaned Out.*
LAUREN FAIRBANKS, *Muzzle Thyself.*
 Sister Carrie.
JUAN FILLOY, *Op Oloop.*
LESLIE A. FIEDLER, *Love and Death in the American Novel.*

GUSTAVE FLAUBERT, *Bouvard and Pécuchet.*
KASS FLEISHER, *Talking out of School.*
FORD MADOX FORD, *The March of Literature.*
JON FOSSE, *Melancholy.*
MAX FRISCH, *I'm Not Stiller.*
 Man in the Holocene.
CARLOS FUENTES, *Christopher Unborn.*
 Distant Relations.
 Terra Nostra.
 Where the Air Is Clear.
JANICE GALLOWAY, *Foreign Parts.*
 The Trick Is to Keep Breathing.
WILLIAM H. GASS, *Cartesian Sonata and Other Novellas.*
 Finding a Form.
 A Temple of Texts.
 The Tunnel.
 Willie Masters' Lonesome Wife.
GÉRARD GAVARRY, *Hoppla! 1 2 3.*
ETIENNE GILSON, *The Arts of the Beautiful.*
 Forms and Substances in the Arts.
C. S. GISCOMBE, *Giscome Road.*
 Here.
 Prairie Style.
DOUGLAS GLOVER, *Bad News of the Heart.*
 The Enamoured Knight.
WITOLD GOMBROWICZ, *A Kind of Testament.*
KAREN ELIZABETH GORDON, *The Red Shoes.*
GEORGI GOSPODINOV, *Natural Novel.*
JUAN GOYTISOLO, *Count Julian.*
 Juan the Landless.
 Makbara.
 Marks of Identity.
PATRICK GRAINVILLE, *The Cave of Heaven.*
HENRY GREEN, *Back.*
 Blindness.
 Concluding.
 Doting.
 Nothing.
JIŘÍ GRUŠA, *The Questionnaire.*
GABRIEL GUDDING, *Rhode Island Notebook.*
JOHN HAWKES, *Whistlejacket.*
ALEKSANDAR HEMON, ED., *Best European Fiction 2010.*
AIDAN HIGGINS, *A Bestiary.*
 Balcony of Europe.
 Bornholm Night-Ferry.
 Darkling Plain: Texts for the Air.
 Flotsam and Jetsam.
 Langrishe, Go Down.
 Scenes from a Receding Past.
 Windy Arbours.
ALDOUS HUXLEY, *Antic Hay.*
 Crome Yellow.
 Point Counter Point.
 Those Barren Leaves.
 Time Must Have a Stop.
MIKHAIL IOSSEL AND JEFF PARKER, EDS., *Amerika:*
 Contemporary Russians View the United States.
GERT JONKE, *Geometric Regional Novel.*
 Homage to Czerny.
 The System of Vienna.
JACQUES JOUET, *Mountain R.*
 Savage.
CHARLES JULIET, *Conversations with Samuel Beckett and*
 Bram van Velde.
MIEKO KANAI, *The Word Book.*
HUGH KENNER, *The Counterfeiters.*
 Flaubert, Joyce and Beckett: The Stoic Comedians.
 Joyce's Voices.
DANILO KIŠ, *Garden, Ashes.*
 A Tomb for Boris Davidovich.
ANITA KONKKA, *A Fool's Paradise.*
GEORGE KONRÁD, *The City Builder.*
TADEUSZ KONWICKI, *A Minor Apocalypse.*
 The Polish Complex.
MENIS KOUMANDAREAS, *Koula.*
ELAINE KRAF, *The Princess of 72nd Street.*
JIM KRUSOE, *Iceland.*
EWA KURYLUK, *Century 21.*
ERIC LAURRENT, *Do Not Touch.*
VIOLETTE LEDUC, *La Bâtarde.*
SUZANNE JILL LEVINE, *The Subversive Scribe:*
 Translating Latin American Fiction.
DEBORAH LEVY, *Billy and Girl.*
 Pillow Talk in Europe and Other Places.
JOSÉ LEZAMA LIMA, *Paradiso.*
ROSA LIKSOM, *Dark Paradise.*
OSMAN LINS, *Avalovara.*
 The Queen of the Prisons of Greece.
ALF MAC LOCHLAINN, *The Corpus in the Library.*
 Out of Focus.
RON LOEWINSOHN, *Magnetic Field(s).*
BRIAN LYNCH, *The Winner of Sorrow.*
D. KEITH MANO, *Take Five.*
MICHELINE AHARONIAN MARCOM, *The Mirror in the Well.*
BEN MARCUS, *The Age of Wire and String.*
WALLACE MARKFIELD, *Teitlebaum's Window.*
 To an Early Grave.
DAVID MARKSON, *Reader's Block.*
 Springer's Progress.
 Wittgenstein's Mistress.
CAROLE MASO, *AVA.*

SELECTED DALKEY ARCHIVE PAPERBACKS

FOR A FULL LIST OF PUBLICATIONS, VISIT:
www.dalkeyarchive.com